Reign of the Buffalo

Reign of the Buffalo

Book 1: The Power of Secrets

Nathan Jay

JNJ Publishing LLC

CONTENTS

CONTENTS

CONTENTS

Southern Comfort

Wilson was playing kickball with his little brother Michael in the front yard when his grandmother stuck her head out of the house and called him.

"Wilson!" she yelled. The boy tossed the ball to his little brother and ran into the house.

"Yes, Grandma?"

"Go across the street to see if Nana Ama is hungry."

"Do I have to? Why can't you send Uncle Charlie?"

"Do as I say, boy. Don't give me any backtalk."

Wilson stomped out of the house.

"Where are you going?" asked Michael as he tried to bounce the ball on his knees. Wilson ignored him and walked out of the yard to the road. After looking both ways, he quickly ran across. Wilson looked back at his brother, kicking the ball carelessly in the afternoon sun.

"Lucky dork," he complained. He didn't understand why Grandma Noya always gave him tasks while Michael was left to frolic amongst the joys of summer. Although he was about to turn thirteen, Wilson didn't appreciate all his grandmother's responsibility.

"Does she think I'm an adult or something?" he mumbled under his breath. A full-grown man was living in the house with them. Wilson's Uncle Charlie spent most of his days in the backroom glued to the tv and rarely came out for anything other than a hot plate of food. Why couldn't he help with some of the chores? Instead, he sat around the house like a log and never lifted a finger.

When the boys visited Grandma Noya's house during the summers, there was always work for Wilson to do. Instead of showering the boy with kisses and gifts like most grandmothers, Grandma Noya gave Wilson a list of chores that seemed to grow longer by the day. From the time his parents disappeared in the sunset until they returned three months later, Grandma Noya leaned on Wilson like he was the man of the house. Never mind the fact that he was only eight years old. From slopping the hogs to helping milk the cows and burning the trash. There wasn't a single day that went by in which his grandmother wasn't applying pressure.

Wilson walked a few feet up the small hill and stopped. Sitting on the hilltop was his great grandmother's house, baking in the Georgia sun.

Both he and his brother Michael hated visiting the house on the other side of the road. The old house was terrifying. There were days when Wilson and his brother sat on his grandmother's porch and watched the evil-looking fortress, waiting on some supernatural event to occur. Sometimes, they'd try to guess how many dead bodies were inside.

The house was the kind of place that haunted children in their dreams. The structure seemed to lean inward and outward in all directions while standing upright in none. Instead of being surrounded by green grass, the house was surrounded by brownish sand, making it seem like the scary place was sitting on an island. The property was surrounded by a badly rotting fence that looked like a giant beast's rotting teeth to the children.

"I hate this shit!" Wilson cursed. He frequently swore when not in adults' presence, which was an excellent time to let the expletives fly. Just like Michael, Wilson was afraid of the house, but he was more afraid of who was inside: his Nana Ama.

Nana Ama lived alone in the old house. She was a Cherokee Native American, and her world within her home was absent of the traditional comforts Wilson enjoyed at the house across the street. There were no tv, radios, or microwaves. Instead, Nana Ama's house had hand-carved furniture, rich multicolored tapestries, and nature paintings. There were only three photos in the place, and all of them had the same two people in them; a much younger Nana Ama standing next to a tall Black man, both with smileless expressions on their faces and standing a few feet apart. The man was her husband, Wilson Jones, who was mysteriously murdered one night on his way home from working in the fields. And although Wilson shared the same name with the man, Grandma Noya instructed him to never speak of him. Ever.

There were no electric appliances in Nana Ama's kitchen. Instead, her kitchen had numerous wooden bowls, strangely shaped utensils, and countless other items that Wilson had never seen. Nana Ama didn't have an electric stove in her kitchen either. She made meals with a giant rusty iron contraption sitting in the middle of the kitchen floor. She heated her oven with wood, which made her house smell like it was perpetually on fire. To Wilson, the place was like walking on a different planet.

Wilson's Great Grandmother's appearance was equally strange to him. Nana Ama's skin was a reddish-bronze color and flawless. There were no wrinkles on her face because she never displayed emotion. Her body was thin without an ounce of fat. Aside from her long silver-gray hair, no one would have ever guessed that she was 104 years old.

But the thing that terrified Wilson the most about Nana Ama was her eyes; one of them was light blue, and the other was cloudy white. When Wilson had first seen Nana Ama's eyes, he screamed and ran out of the room. Looking into Nana Ama's white eye made Wilson feel like hundreds of little worms were crawling beneath his skin. Later his grandmother tried to assure him that Nana Ama's eyeball was just a normal one.

"Nana Ama is blind out of that eye," his grandmother told him. "She got hit in the eye with a rock when she was a child, and her eye changed color because she lost her vision."

But Wilson knew better. There was something unnatural about Nana Ama, and he didn't care what his grandmother said. His great-grandmother wasn't like everyone else, and the old woman scared him to his core.

Nana Ama spent all her days alone in the house. There were no maids or helpers who visited. Only her daughter, Grandma Noya, went to the home three times per day to make meals for her. Day after day, Nana Ama sat alone in her bedroom, staring out into the dark forest at the edge of the backyard.

"Grandma, why does Nana Ama stay in that big house alone?" Wilson had asked after seeing his Great Grandmother.

"She likes the quiet," Grandma Noya replied. "The noise of the world upsets her."

Indeed, the old woman was quiet. In the four summers that Wilson and Michael had visited, Wilson had only heard her speak twice. Once, when a doctor came to the house to check her blood pressure. Another when Grandma Noya had threatened a man from the IRS.

"Go or die," Nana Ama had said to the White businessman. The sound of her voice was worse than her appearance; it was deep and forceful. Wisely, the man backed out of the room and never returned.

Wilson opened the old gate and stumbled across the sandy yard to the front porch. He knocked on the old door before turning the knob to open it. Wilson stuck his head into the damp house to announce his arrival.

"Nana Ama? It's Wilson. I'm coming in, okay?" he yelled. His voice echoed through the empty house like an open well. There was no response. After taking a deep breath, Wilson walked into the house and closed the door behind him. Taking giant steps, he walked quickly to the rear of the house where Nana Ama's bedroom was.

"Nana Ama? Can I come in?" he asked after knocking on the large wooden door. He knew his Great Grandmother wouldn't respond, yet he announced his presence anyway. Grandma Noya told him it was rude for a man to enter a woman's bedroom without revealing his intentions.

"I'm coming in now, okay?" he said. Slowly, he pushed the door open. Usually, Nana Ama would be seated in the large rocking chair in front of the window. This time the rocking chair was empty. Instead, he saw the old woman's figure through the sheer canopy curtains. She was lying in bed.

"Nana Ama?" Wilson asked. "Grandma Noya wanted me to tell you that she's coming over to cook lunch for you. Are you hungry?"

She didn't respond. Wilson walked to the side of the bed. He gently pushed aside the sheer curtain to look at his Great Grandmother. She seemed to be sleeping. Her long silver hair spread out across the pillows. Wilson could see that although Nana Ama was lying underneath the blanket, she was fully dressed. He recognized the dress she was wearing – her wedding dress; he'd seen Nana Ama wearing it in the photo in the living room.

"Nana Ama?" asked Wilson as he moved closer. He started to feel nervous. He couldn't see his Great Grandmother's chest moving up and down. Cautiously, he placed his hand above her face to see if he could feel her breath.

Suddenly the old woman's hand shot up and locked on Wilson's wrist. The child screamed out in surprise. He tried to let go, but Nana Ama wouldn't release him.

"Please, Nana! It hurts!" he cried out. The old woman's eyes opened wide, and she turned to look at Wilson.

"The buffalo! You must bring forth their spirits!" she hissed. Wilson struggled to pull his arm away, but his Great Grandmother's grip was like a vice. Wilson tried to fall to the floor so that she would let go. Instead of releasing his arm, Nana Ama's grip tightened, her long finger-nails dug into Wilson's skin.

"Aaaaahhh! Let me go!"

The woman's eyes focused on the child's eyes. Wilson could feel his heart pounding heavily in his chest. Soon he was struggling to breathe.

As he dangled above the floor, his Great Grandmother began cackling out loud.

"Please...Please..." begged Wilson. He was becoming lightheaded. Drool started to pour out of his mouth. With her right hand, Nana Ama placed her palm across his right eye and forehead. The room began to get dark to Wilson. He was seconds from passing out when his Great Grandmother dropped him on the floor. He didn't stand up. Instead, he crawled towards the door, terrified. Nana Ama threw back the blankets and walked towards the boy as he crawled towards the front door.

"The evil is coming from the underworld. You must protect!"

Wilson stopped crawling away. Instead, he curled up in a ball on the floor and covered his ears.

"Grandma Noya! Help!"

Nana Ama stood above him with her white eye staring into Wilson's face. Finally, she took a deep breath and smiled.

"My Wilson. I have chosen well."

The old woman collapsed in the middle of the bedroom with her eyes open. Wilson didn't wait around to see if she was alive. He sprinted out of the house to get his Grandma Noya.

2

Summer's Eye

Two weeks after Nana Ama's funeral, Wilson and his little brother returned to Washington, DC, with their parents. The school year was about to start, and the boys were exhausted from all their summer activities. Under his father's strict eye, Wilson did as he usually did; he started doing math problems from the previous year to refresh his memory. It was an old trick his dad had taught him to "forget the dumbness of Summer." After pulling out his math book from the previous school year, Wilson sat at the dining room table. Soon his dad entered the room.

"I have to go to the supermarket with your mother," said Wilson's father. "Be sure you finish those math problems. I'll be checking as soon as we return."

"Okay, Dad."

Suddenly Wilson's little brother ran into the room.

"Hey, Dad! Can you bring me some candy back from the store? Please?" begged Michael. His mother walked into the room and grabbed her keys from the counter.

"Now you know we're not getting that. You ate enough candy during your visit to your grandmother's. There's a bowl of fruit on the table. Eat an apple instead."

Michael flopped down at the dining room table and grabbed an apple from the fruit bowl. As his father walked past, he whispered in the boy's ear.

"A candy bar, right?"

Michael shook his head and smiled.

"Me too, Dad," whispered Wilson. His Dad winked at him before walking out of the room.

As soon as the boys' mother and father left, Michael took advantage and interrupted his brother's studies.

"Hey, Wilson."

"What?"

"Let's play football on the video game."

"I can't. You just heard Dad tell me he's going to check my work when he comes back."

"It's just a quick game. Come on."

"No. School starts next week, and Dad will be mad for sure."

"You're a chicken shit. Scared that I'll whip your ass like I always do."

"You only won the last game by luck."

"You wish."

"Then prove it."

Wilson delayed studying to play games with his little brother. After losing one game to Michael and beating him in two others, Wilson returned to his studies. When he finished, he went to his bedroom to read a magazine. That is when he started to have trouble with his right eye.

It started with his eye being watery. As he read his magazine, his eyeball filled with water and dripped down his cheek. After wiping the tears away, he felt a tingling sensation just beneath the eyelid. Wilson assumed that he had gotten dirt in his eye somehow and didn't make much of it. But the next day, when he woke up, his pillow was drenched as if he'd been crying the whole night. He went to his mother and father to complain, and they told him to rinse his eye out.

"You're playing too many video games. Get some rest, and you'll be fine."

On the third day, it was worse. Wilson had to walk around with a paper towel to wipe away all the tears coming from his eye. Still resigned to the fact that too many video games were affecting his eyes, Wilson's parents didn't think much of it. But by the time evening arrived, his eyeball was pink. Wilson's mother got on the phone and made an emergency appointment. The next day they took him to an eye doctor. After looking inside Wilson's eye, the doctor agreed that video games were the culprit.

"We see this a lot when summer ends. Kids spend three months in front of the tv on those video games. It's unhealthy, and eventually, their eyes object by developing irritations. No worries, though. We'll prescribe an antibiotic and eyedrops. That should stop the problem right away," the doctor said to his mom.

But Wilson's eye didn't get better. One month later, in addition to the eyeball being watery, it became bloodshot. This time his parents took him to the ophthalmologist to check for an infection. After running a battery of tests, the doctor couldn't find anything wrong with Wilson's eye. Wilson stood in front of a vision chart and scored 20/20 on his vision test.

"I'm sorry, ma'am," the doctor explained. "Other than a little irritation, there doesn't seem to be anything wrong with his eye. They're perfectly normal."

Wilson's mother relaxed a bit after visiting the doctor. She made sure Wilson covered the eye with clean gauze before he showered and forbade him from playing video games. Still, the eyeball continued dripping with tears and remained red.

On the second month after his first visit to the doctor, Wilson noticed a difference in his vision. A red line sometimes appeared and outlined whatever he was watching. Realizing that his parents were already on edge, Wilson kept the secret to himself and went about his daily activities as if nothing were wrong. But it wasn't long before a new problem arose - he began to lose sleep. Although Wilson closed his eyes to sleep at night, his eyelid would suddenly pop open, interrupting his slumber and forcing him to stay awake for hours. On the third night of getting only a few hours of sleep, Wilson had no choice but to reveal his secret.

"What do you mean *open*?" his mother asked when he went to her with the issue.

"I mean open. I can still see everything in the room."

"Come here. Let me look at your eye."

After flushing his eye with eyedrops, his mother pried open his eyelid to look at his eyeball.

"Dustin!" she yelled out. "Come here!"

Wilson's father rushed into the room.

"What is it?"

"Look at his eye!"

Dustin looked into Wilson's eye and jumped. His ordinarily brown iris had a white dot in the center of it.

"What is that?" asked Wilson's father.

"We need to get you to the doctor today," his mother replied.

Wilson returned to the doctor for the third time, but the doctor couldn't explain the color change.

"We've run tests for pigmentary glaucoma, iris melanoma, and Horner's syndrome. All the tests have returned negative," the doctor explained to Wilson's mother and father.

"But something isn't right. You can see discoloration," replied Wilson's mother. "And just this morning, he complained about the eye being unable to remain closed when he sleeps."

"Well, we can run an MRI if you want, but I don't think it's MS or Tourette's. Let's have you monitor him while he sleeps tonight."

As the family drove home, Wilson's parents whispered in the front seat. Wilson and his brother pretended to be asleep but instead were listening to the conversation.

"This is weird."

"Yes, but I think you're making too big an issue of it. Boys will be boys. When she was a little girl, Nana Ama's eye..."

Julia's face grew white, and a worried look appeared on her face.

"Oh, my God! I forgot! Nana Ama's eye! What if Wilson has the same problem? What if it's hereditary? Maybe we should turn around and go back to inform the doctor."

"Inform him of what? My Grandmother's condition? Nana Ama's eye was a different thing altogether. The doctor ran all the necessary tests on Wilson. If the problem were serious, Dr. Montgomery would've informed us. Stop overreacting."

"But what if he missed something, Dustin. You know these doctors screw up every day. What if..."

Dustin looked in the rearview mirror and saw both his sons staring at them.

"Let's talk about this at home, okay?"

"But if we..."

"Let's discuss this at home," Dustin repeated while nodding at the kids. "Not now."

But Wilson and Michael already knew what their mother was going to say to their dad. They had seen the same thing too – in Nana Ama's eye.

"Dude. I'm going to start calling you the New Nana," Michael whispered. The little boy leaned against the window of the car and started cracking up laughing. But Wilson wasn't laughing. He remembered how Nana Ama had touched his face before she died.

"Shut up, you little piss," Wilson snapped.

"I heard that. Cut the crap," yelled Dustin from the front seat.

Wilson and Michael stayed home from school for the remainder of the day while their parents took sick days away from work. While Wilson's mother spent the day on the internet researching possible causes for her son's ailment, his father sat watching the football game, mostly unfazed by the change in Wilson's eye. At bedtime, Wilson's mother decided to sleep in the same room with the children.

"Close your eyes," she said after turning out the lights. "Are your eyes completely closed?"

"Yes."

"Do you see anything?"

"No."

Julia walked over to look at her son. Both of Wilson's eyes remained shut. She slid into bed with him, and they both fell asleep.

In the morning, Wilson woke up to a funny sensation in his eye. He rubbed it, and his eyelid started itching so bad that he almost lifted the eyelid to scratch his eyeball with his nail. His mother was gone, so Wilson didn't need to worry about her telling him not to touch it. With two fingers, he grabbed the eyelid and lifted it. Just as he did, he felt something moving on his eyelid that felt like worms. Wilson jumped out of bed and rushed to the bathroom mirror. He opened his eyelid and looked at his eyeball. All the color in his eye was gone. The whole eyeball was completely white! Surprised, Wilson stumbled back and almost fell. Slowly, he walked back to the mirror for a second look. After opening his eyelid again, he stared at the white iris.

Something on it moved!

Thinking he imagined something, Wilson blinked and opened his eyelid to look again. He watched in horror as he saw what looked to be a white worm crawl across his eyeball.

"Mom!" he yelled. His mother rushed into the bathroom.

"What is it?"

"Something's in there! Just now! I saw it!"

His mother took his face into her hands and looked at his eye.

"Oh my God!" she yelled. "Dustin!"

In seconds, Wilson's father and brother crowded in the bathroom with Wilson and his mom.

"His whole Iris is white!"

The parents took their son to the eye doctor again. After running more tests, the doctor found the same result.

"I'm sorry. There's no explanation for the color change. From what we see, the eye is healthy."

"That can't be. A person's iris doesn't just change color for no reason."

"From what our tests reveal, his eye is normal."

"But he's complaining that he saw something crawling across his eyeball. He says he saw a white worm."

"We've run blood tests and performed MRI's. Nothing is there. And with the antibiotics and medicated eyedrops, nothing could evade detection. I guess that he has a bit of an overactive imagination. Worms couldn't evade detection. Not in his eye. He's healthy."

Julia exploded.

"My son is not healthy, Goddamn it! His eye is almost completely white! Do your fucking job!"

The doctor restrained himself and started writing on his notepad.

"I'm going to give you a referral. Dr. Williamson is top-notch in his field."

The doctor passed the referral form to Julia. She grabbed Wilson by the hand and stormed out of the doctor's office.

3

Next Summer's Visions

Wilson sat in the back of the class, bored out of his mind. There were only three more days until summer, and he would be returning to see his grandmother. Wilson lifted the superhero eyepatch his mother had purchased for him online and rubbed his eye. He appreciated that his mother cared about how the students stared at him, but the eyepatch made him feel like he was wearing a blanket on his face.

Finally, the teacher interrupted the classroom with an announcement.

"Okay, class. Summer's almost here and..."

Before the teacher could finish her sentence, the classroom erupted in celebration.

"All right. All right. Calm down," said the overweight middle-aged woman. "We only have three more days of school, but I have one final project for you."

This time, the students verbally complained.

"I think you all are going to like this. Over the weekend, what I want you to do is to write a one-page report on what you plan on doing for the summer."

A chubby red-haired boy turned around and whispered to Wilson.

"We know what One-Eye will be doing for summer. Robbing a ship."

The group of students surrounding Wilson all started giggling and got the attention of the teacher.

"Excuse me. Jared O'Brien. Do you have something you want to share with the rest of the class?"

"No, Mrs. Harrell."

Wilson took the eyepatch off and rubbed his eye. As the students turned around to stare at him, Wilson felt a warm sensation in his head. Jared gave him a disgusted look before making another comment.

"Wow. Ghost-eye."

The group of students started giggling again and continued staring at Wilson.

That is when it happened.

Wilson watched in astonishment as Jared's body began to glow bright red. Orange sparks sprayed throughout the room like embers from a forest. Wilson watched in horror as the boy's skin began to blister on his forehead. Soon his red hair burst into flames. Seemingly unaware of what was happening, the boy continued staring at Wilson. Soon a glowing white dot appeared in the center of the child's forehead. Like a laser, the white mark carved a line through the center of his face. Wilson was terrified. He couldn't take his eyes off his classmate. The sound of the teacher's voice floated through the fire like a whisper.

"Wilson. Would you mind telling the rest of the class what you and Mr. O'Brien find so entertaining?"

But Wilson couldn't respond. The glowing sparks caused the desks, the floor, and the ceiling to burst into flames. Billows of black smoke smothered the classroom causing Wilson to cough. He frantically searched the room, looking for the teacher, but the smoke was too thick. The room was on fire. All the other students were blurs. The only person Wilson could see through the heat was Jared, a glowing red line down the center of his partially blistered face. One side of his body was frozen in ice while the other half was bright red as if a fire were burning within him. There was a flash of white light, and the boy's skin began to stretch like taffy, all the while, a sinister smile on Jared's face. Suddenly his demonic voice began to speak.

"Tomorrow, I'll dare Devon Miller to run across the street during heavy traffic. He'll try it and get hit by a gas truck. The truck will explode. Four people will die. It'll all be your fault because you didn't do anything to stop me."

Wilson was transfixed. He watched as both sides of Jared's face began to move independently of one another like waves in an ocean.

"Killing Devon will be my first murder, but it won't be the last. I'll kill again. And Again. And again."

"No," whispered Wilson.

"In a few years, I'll rob a store. When my mother threatens to report me to the police, I'll put rat poison in her coffee and kill her. I'll keep killing because you never stopped me! It'll be your fault! You!"

"You can't. I have to stop you!" whispered Wilson.

"You can't stop me. I'll kill, and it'll be your fault!"

There was another flash of white light, and Wilson blinked. Suddenly he was on the floor, overwhelmed with confusion and blurry shapes. After a while, his vision came back. Students surrounded him; Jared stood above him, staring at him with his mouth open. The teacher was standing over him, tapping him lightly on his face.

"Sally, go to the Principal's office and tell them we need to call the paramedics."

Wilson attempted to sit up, but his teacher pushed him back to the floor.

"Relax, Wilson. Relax."

"You have to stop him. He's going to kill someone. Jared is evil."

Wilson was in a state of panic. He'd heard the demonic confessions of his classmate, and he had to stop it. Suddenly he saw Jared's face standing in the large circle surrounding him, a sick smile on his face.

"Look at him! He's going to do it! He's a murderer!"

"Relax, Wilson. You hit your head on the edge of the desk."

"You don't understand," he continued. "Jared is a killer."

The words shook the teacher, and she tried to talk over Wilson to hide what he was saying from the other students. But the terrified looks on the students' faces revealed that his words had registered with them. They all began whispering to one another while standing over Wilson.

"Shhhh...relax. Help is on the way."

Wilson lay his head back on the classroom floor. He felt something wet on his eye. When he reached up to wipe it away, he saw his hand. Blood was all over it.

4

Nobody Knows

Dustin looked over at his son and gave him a weak smile.

"No worries. We'll be home in a little while," Wilson's father said as he tried to drive while keeping a close watch on his son. But Wilson wasn't paying attention. He was looking out of the passenger window, trying to process what his classmate Jared had told him.

"The school nurse says you're going to be okay. Just a slight concussion and a couple of stitches from hitting your head on the corner of the desk."

Wilson turned to his dad.

"Are we still going to Grandma's for the summer?"

"Yeah. I think so. Grandma Noya seems to think city life and pollution is getting to you."

"That's all you think it is?"

"What were you doing in that classroom?"

"What do you mean?"

"You don't remember getting out of your seat and taking a swing at your classmate?"

"No."

"Well, your teacher said you did."

"I don't remember that."

"She said you were going on and on about your classmate being a murderer. Where did you get that?"

"I don't know, Dad. It might be my eye. It's making me see things that..."

Dustin quickly changed the subject.

"Anyway...you guys are going to see your Grandma again for the summer. It'll do you and your brother good to get out of this mess for a while."

Wilson sighed.

"What's the matter? You don't want to go?"

"Grandma Noya always makes me work. There's no rest for me."

Dustin started laughing.

"I know you won't believe me, but I went through that same workload year after year. When you get older, you'll have a better appreciation for it. Believe me."

"I don't think so."

"You watch. Right now, you hate the smell of Grandma Noya's slop bucket and the sounds the pigs make when you pour it in the trough. But in time, you won't even focus on those things. Instead, you'll remember the sounds of the roosters and the crickets. You'll remember the dew-covered grass in the mornings as you go to the chicken coop to collect the eggs. Watch. Georgia is heaven during the summertime. You're just too young to appreciate it."

Dustin parked the car, and both he and Wilson climbed out. As they climbed out of the car, Dustin tugged on Wilson's sleeve.

"Hey. Don't bring up your eye to your mother. You know how she gets."

"Okay."

As soon as they arrived at the front door, Julia swung it open.

"Ouch!" she said as soon as she saw the bump on the side of Wilson's head. "Does it hurt?"

"Not that much," he replied as he tried to walk past her. Julia stopped him and lifted his head.

"How's your eye?"

"I didn't hit my eye, mom. I hit my head on the corner of the desk."

"Your eye is okay?"

"Yes. It's fine. I just tripped."

"Go to the bedroom and lie down. I'll bring you some soup a little later."

Wilson walked into his bedroom and flopped down on his bed. His little brother was sitting on the bed opposite him.

"You okay, bro?"

"I'm good."

"Mom was freaking out. She's been on the phone with doctors since we got home. You're about to be the biggest pin cushion on earth."

"Shut up, dummy."

"You know we're going back to Grandma Noya's for the summer, right?"

"Yeah. Dad already told me."

"Mom's against it. She thinks it's something around there that messed up your eye."

"Really? What do you think?"

"I think Dad knows something. Why isn't he worrying like mom?"

"Yeah. I think Dad knows something too. Just when we came into the house, he told me not to tell mom anything about my eye."

"That's weird. Oh well, at least we get to go to Grandma Noya's again."

"Good for you, maybe. For me, it's a bunch of yard work."

"Sucks to be you. I guess grandma's going to put you to work again."

"I guess."

Wilson laid down and closed his eyes. Seconds later, he was snoring.

The next day he stayed at home. Although the lump on Wilson's head had shrunk considerably, his mother thought it best if he stayed home. Wilson didn't complain about it. He remembered the book report Mrs. Harrell assigned to the class, and he smiled. Based on how jittery his mother was about his condition, Wilson figured he could milk one more day at home out of his injury.

As soon as his family left the house for the day, Wilson ran to the kitchen and emptied half a box of cereal into one of his mother's large mixing bowls. After drowning the cereal in milk, he went to the den and turned on the tv. Wilson intended to find his favorite cartoon channel and watch his fill until he became sleepy. Instead, he flipped through news channels.

Finally, he stopped.

There it was.

"Welcome to News 10. I'm Lynda Smith. We have breaking news. Let's go to Nick Willis on the scene at Foxhall and Jonesborough, where there's been a major explosion. Hello Nick. What can you tell us about this accident?"

"Hello, Lynda. As you can see, there's been a massive explosion here at the intersection of Foxhall and Jonesborough involving multiple cars and a gasoline truck. The Police Department, Hazmat crews, and the Fire department are all on the scene for what looks to be one of the deadliest accidents in recent memory. Several witnesses tell us that they saw children attempting to cross the intersection around the same time the explosion occurred. No confirmation if those children were involved in the accident, but we're expecting an update from the Fire Chief and the Detective momentarily. Stay tuned as we bring you further details on this horrific accident. This is Nick Willis at News 10. Lynda, back to you."

Wilson dropped his spoon in his bowl and turned off the tv.

"It's Jared. I know it."

After sitting on the sofa watching the blank tv for a few minutes, Wilson went to the kitchen and dumped his cereal in the sink. He walked into the bathroom and stared at his eye in the mirror.

"Is it just my imagination? Is my mind playing tricks on me? Did Jared kill those people?"

Wilson pulled back his eyelid and looked at his eye again. Once again, a white wormlike creature shot across his eyeball. After seeing the worm, Wilson began to feel sick. He went to his bed to lie down and didn't wake up until his family returned home.

5

Jared

Michael bounced the ball on the street as Wilson watched him from the porch. Wilson laughed as his brother threw up the ball at the basketball goal and missed.

"You suck!" Wilson yelled from the porch. "Stop messing around so we can go to the store."

"I'm better than you," Michael responded before spinning around to attempt a jump shot.

"No, you're not."

"Come down and prove it, smart ass. If I win, you have to buy me whatever I want at the store."

"And if you lose?"

"I'll buy you whatever you want."

"With what money? You're broke."

"Okay, what if I clean the room for a month?"

Wilson stood up. He was about to go down to challenge his brother when a couple of boys encircled Michael on their bikes.

"Hey, Mike! You want to play horse?" asked Tristan, the blond-haired boy who lived across the street from them. Michael bounced the ball a couple of times and shook his head.

"Nah, I'm not in the mood today. Wilson and I are about to ride to the store."

"Oh yeah? Can we roll with you?" asked Sean, Tristan's twin brother.

Michael stopped bouncing the ball and yelled to Wilson.

"Wilson! Are you ready to go to the store?"

"Yeah! Let me get my bike!"

Wilson went into the garage to retrieve his bike. A few minutes later, all four boys rode down the street on their way to the convenience store.

When they arrived at the store, all four boys parked their bikes on the side of the building.

"Hey, Tristan, what are you getting?" asked Sean. "Dad only gave me five dollars."

"I'll probably get some gummy bears, chips, and a soda. Mom gave me ten dollars," replied Tristan.

Michael stood at the entrance of the store, digging in his pockets while his brother smiled. Wilson knew Michael didn't have money, and he prepared himself for what came next.

"Hey, Wilson. Do you..."

Wilson interrupted him.

"A soda and chips, or chips and candy. But you can't have everything."

"Cool."

Wilson and Michael walked into the convenience store and headed to the candy rack. After struggling to decide, Wilson grabbed some jawbreakers and a soda. Michael's eyes shifted between his favorite candy, the bags of chips, and the refrigerated sodas against the wall.

"Hurry up, Michael. We don't have all day."

Michael stuck up his middle finger at Wilson and grabbed his favorite bag of candy and soda. As the two boys headed to the register, Wilson froze. Standing in front of the counter was the boy from his class, Jared.

"Bro, why are you stopping? Aren't you going to pay for our stuff?" asked Michael while opening his bag of candy. But Wilson could do nothing but stare. He remembered what the news said about the accident. Jared killed someone. Slowly, Wilson walked up to the counter to pay for his items.

"Old Ghost Eye. What's a scrub like you doing out?" asked Jared as he smirked at Wilson.

"What do you think I'm doing?" replied Wilson while waiting his turn.

"How's that peeper? Are you still seeing wild shit?"

Michael stepped from behind Wilson and looked at the plump teenager.

"Who the fuck's this lard ass?" he asked. Wilson smiled. He knew Michael would hear the conversation and jump in. Michael had a bad temper. Meanwhile, Tristan and Sean stood in the back of the line and snickered at Michael's comment. Jared frowned at the two boys and turned his attention to Michael.

"Are you the pirate's wife or little brother? I can't tell the difference," Jared replied.

"You'd better watch your mouth before I knock your teeth out," growled Wilson. He was just as protective of Michael as his little brother was of him.

"Hey, it's not my fault your psycho eyeball is making your whole family nuts."

Wilson moved close to Jared and grabbed his arm. He lowered his voice and whispered.

"I know it was you, fat boy. You killed those people over on Jonesborough. Don't think I won't go to the cops about it."

"Hey...I don't know what you're talking about."

"You do know, fat boy. And if you fuck with me, I'll tell the world what I saw."

"You're crazy, man. Let go of my arm."

The group of boys watched in astonishment as Jared started trembling in fear. Suddenly, he dropped his bag of candy on the floor and took off running out of the store. Michael stared at his brother with his mouth open.

"Dude! What did you say to him?"

Wilson ignored the question and rushed to pay for his candy.

"Hey Sean and Tristan, we'll catch up with you guys later."

Wilson grabbed Michael's arm, and they rushed out the door. He looked down the road and saw Jared pedaling away on his bike. Wilson turned to Michael.

"Go home and wait for me to come back."

"Where are you going?"

"I'm going to check on Fat Boy. I think he's up to something."

"No, man. We shouldn't be splitting up."

"Ride back with Tristan and Sean if you want to."

"What if mom asks where you are?"

"I don't know. Just tell mom I stopped to get a nail out of my bicycle tire."

"How long are you going to be?"

"Ten minutes, maybe shorter."

Wilson sped out of the parking lot behind Jared. He didn't know how he was going to do it, but he had to stop him.

Jared rode on for several minutes before turning on Rosemary lane. He cut between two houses and rode rudely across one of the resident's yard.

"Hey, you little shit! Get off my lawn!" screamed an elderly man.

"Get fucked!" Jared replied and sped on. As he sped on, Wilson too cut through the man's yard. The man was going back into the house, so the man didn't see Wilson do it. Jared sped on until he reached a steep hill. Jared stopped and looked around. His eyes lit up when he saw Wilson.

"You following me, Black Beard? You're too chick shit to go down this hill."

Wilson continued pedaling ahead as Jared descended. Wilson paused. Jared wasn't lying. He was terrified to go down after the boy. Finally, after Jared reached the bottom, Wilson took a deep breath and began to roll down the hill. The ride was bumpier than he expected. Wilson's handlebars shook as the bike accelerated. He pressed the brakes intermittently to try to slow himself, but he was still going down the hill faster than he liked. Jared stopped at the bottom of the hill with his arms folded.

"I've got to see this idiot crash," he shouted. "Go ahead, you one-eyed idiot! Crash!"

Wilson maintained his control and focused. As he reached the bottom of the hill, Jared climbed on his bike and took off pedaling.

"Lucky fuck!" he yelled.

As Wilson slowed his bike, he felt something hit him in his face. Like a reflex, both hands went to his eye, forgetting he was supposed to be steering the bike. Wilson flew over the handlebars and tumbled into the grass. When he finally stopped rolling, he stood up and looked around. The sun was gone. Confused and blinking furiously, Wilson wiped at his eye, trying to correct his vision. After a few moments, he realized that the issue wasn't his eyes. The sun was gone. Everything was as dark as midnight. He could see Jared riding ahead of him onto the railroad tracks. Suddenly the boy stopped pedaling.

"What the fuck?" Jared asked. "Am I imagining this?"

He dropped his bike onto the railroad tracks and looked around.

Wilson remained calm. A warm feeling moved through his chest like a sip of hot chocolate. His face felt bubbly around his eye like someone had poured soda onto his skull. He began to sense things all around him; he heard crickets singing and various insects buzzing as they flew around him.

"What's happening to me?" Wilson whispered. He took in a deep break and exhaled. The air tasted sweet as it filled his lungs. Gently, he took a small step; the ground felt like a soft mattress under his feet. Wilson looked around and realized his vision had changed. Now he could see things with such clarity that it scared him. He could see the approaching train that was so far away that it hadn't sounded its horn yet.

"How am I able to see that far?" Wilson whispered.

Finally, his eyes fell on Jared.

"Are you seeing this?" Jared yelled to Wilson.

Something struck Wilson like a bolt of electricity. He remembered what Jared had told him when they were in class. He remembered the carnage on the news. There was evil in Jared, and he was the only person that knew what his intentions were.

"I know what you did, Jared. I know who you killed."

Jared's eyes widened.

"Hey! Shut up!"

Wilson continued revealing what he knew.

"I even know the person you killed."

"I said shut up, you fucking freak!"

"Devon is the kid's name."

Jared was startled.

"Wait. How do you..."

"I know you hate your mom too. You're going to put rat poison in her drink."

"How do you know that?"

"I know it all, Jared. You're not going to get away with this."

Jared grabbed his bike and hopped on.

"Stay away from me, you freak!"

Suddenly the sound of the train's horn blared, and both boys turned to look. Jared began pedaling his bike towards the track to cross over. Without thinking, Wilson waved his arm in the air. The bicycle went flying into the bushes while Jared landed squarely on the railroad tracks.

"Ahhhhh!" he screamed as the train became visible at the other end of the field.

"Hey! You gotta help me!" Jared begged. "I can't move my legs."

Wilson barely heard the boy's words. The whole world was a whisper to him, and he could only see the horrible things that Jared planned to do. His arm remained extended as his fingers formed an open claw.

"Wilson! Help me! I'm stuck!"

After realizing that the boy wouldn't help him, Jared crawled along the tracks until he was off. He attempted to stand up but fell hopelessly to the ground.

"What's happening?" Jared cried out. The more the boy tried to free himself, the tighter Wilson squeezed his hand.

"I know what you're going to do," Wilson whispered. He was unaware that he was holding the boy in place for the train. Jared's eyes widened as the train drew closer.

"Mommy!" he screamed. But the only person that could hear him was Wilson.

Just as the train was about to smash into Jared's body, Wilson jerked his arm back. The boy's body slid off the tracks, but his legs remained.

"Ahhhhh!"

Jared screamed out in agony as the train severed his legs from his body. The scream brought Wilson back to reality. He looked for Jared lying on the track, but the train was too long, and it blocked his vision. Wilson grabbed his bike, climbed up the hill, and went home.

6

Mom's Secret

The rumble of thunder raised Wilson from his sleep, and he sat up in his bed to look around the room. Although he could hear Michael snoring through the noise of the thunderstorm, the flashes of lightning gave his bedroom an eerie glow that made him afraid. He laid back down and tried to return to sleep. Wilson kept seeing Jared lying on the railroad tracks, begging for help. The boy's screams kept echoing through his dreams. Something happened to Wilson, and he wasn't sure what to make of it. There was a certain amount of satisfaction in seeing a "big mouth" suffer, but no one deserved what Jared got. For a moment, Wilson wiggled his toes and tried to imagine what life would be like if he didn't have legs. Frustrated with his imagination and the guilt he felt, he closed his eyes and tried to sleep again.

The rolling sound of the thunderstorm denied his attempts, and once again, he sat up in bed staring into the darkness. After a few moments, Wilson noticed a soft light shining underneath his bedroom door. Wilson climbed out of bed, inched open his bedroom door, and walked down the hall. The light came from the den, which meant either his mother or father was there watching tv. After stopping for a drink of water in the kitchen, he decided he'd see who it was.

As he got closer to the den, he noticed that the door wasn't completely closed. He could see his mom dozing off on the sofa while her favorite news show played on the television. Wilson paused to listen to the news correspondent. The police still hadn't found a cause for the accident, but Wilson knew the outcome. Slowly, he pushed the door open.

Suddenly his eye began to itch. Remembering the white worm crawling across his eyeball, Wilson rubbed it lightly. Then his eye started itching so much that he rubbed it again – hard. As soon as he touched the door, he began to see orange embers of fire floating around the room. As if sensing his presence, his mother stood and turned to face him. Her hair burst into flame, sending billows of smoke towards the ceiling.

"My son," Julia said, unaware of the flame at the top of her head. A white dot began glowing in the center of her forehead. Just as Wilson had witnessed in school, a white laser began burning in a straight line down the center of his mother's face and neck. Soon both sides of her face stretched the skin like rubber but remained connected.

"Why are you here? I never wanted you! Never!" her demonic voice yelled. "I can't wait to leave the three of you! I wish you all would die!"

Wilson's eyes filled with tears, and he began backing away. The evil monster that was his mother continued.

"Your father isn't the only man in my life. The neighbor living on the edge of our block is my lover," she said with a cold, detached look on her face. Wilson's eyes widened, and he began sobbing. His mother took another step in his direction.

"Yes. Richard McConnell has been my lover for years. Michael is only half your brother. Richard is his father."

Tears began flowing down Wilson's face. He wanted to say something, but he couldn't. His mouth didn't know how to speak the words. Still, his mother moved closer.

"You had a sister, but I didn't want her. I had an abortion."

The smell of the burned hair began to choke Wilson, and he coughed; the sound echoed in the house as if he were in a dream.

"This summer, I will abandon you. Richard and I will go to London, and you will never see me again! I want the three of you out of my life!"

Suddenly, Julia's face burst into a bluish flame. Like wax, all the skin melted off her face revealing a skull. She reached out to touch Wilson, and he jumped. There was a loud popping sound and a flash of white light. Suddenly he was standing in the middle of the den with his mother holding his arm.

"Wilson! You okay?" his mother asked. Wilson looked confused.

"I'm...okay...I think."

"Are you sure? You were standing there for a little while without moving."

"I'm okay, mom. I just came to see why the television was on. I'm fine."

"Are you sure? How's your eye?"

"It's fine, mom. Really."

"Okay. I'm going to bed now."

Julia tried to touch her son's face, but he moved away. Wilson was still trying to process what his mom had told him. Was he hallucinating? Did his mother abort his unborn sister? And what about his brother? He and Michael were only half-brothers? Wilson's head was spinning.

"Goodnight, mom," he said before turning and walking quickly back to his bedroom.

"Goodnight, baby. See you tomorrow," his mom responded.

Wilson went into his bedroom and laid down on his bed. The images of his mother were so vivid in his mind that he couldn't sleep. He looked over at his brother, fast asleep in the bed beside him. Wilson raised the covers over his head and began to cry. What if what he had seen was true? Did he and his brother have different fathers? Wilson started thinking about all the Thanksgiving celebrations and Christmases his family had shared. The numerous summers they spent playing in the fields at his grandmother's house. Was it all a lie? He began to comb through all the times his mother spent on her phone, all the separate business trips she had away from them, what she did on her days off when she was at home alone. His mother had fooled them all. And she would leave them by the end of the summer. She'd rip apart the world of her family just to be selfish with the jerk down the street.

By the time the sun came up, Wilson's eyelids were heavy. Two more days and he and his brother would be going back down South. He had to do something to change the trajectory of the approaching events. Wilson climbed out of bed and went into the bathroom to take a shower. When he finished, he brushed his teeth and got dressed. Before anyone else had awakened, he quietly opened the front door and walked onto the porch. Wilson stood at the edge of his front yard, looking down the street. As soon as he spotted his target, he began his walk towards the man that wanted to destroy his family.

7

Family Defense

"Wilson! How's it going? You're out for an early walk this morning?"

The athletic middle-aged man dressed in a terrycloth robe bent over in his driveway to pick up his morning newspaper.

"I'm fine, Mr. McConnell. Thanks," replied Wilson as he walked close to the man's driveway. He couldn't believe his mother chose Richard to have an affair. He reminded Wilson of one of those men that fought old age by wearing teenaged clothing and blaring hip hop music.

"What a loser," Wilson whispered underneath his breath. The man flashed a smile and untangled his lawn sprinkler.

"I heard you guys are going to your grandmother's again this summer. Summer's a nice time to travel, isn't it?"

"What do you mean?"

"I mean, you and your brother are lucky. Adults are stuck working year-round in jobs they hate. Kids have it so good. I'd give anything to have the summer off. You guys are heading down South to see your grandmother again, am I right?"

"How do you know that?"

Wilson looked at the man suspiciously. There was only one way the man could've known where he and his brother were going for the summer – his mother.

"Oh, word gets around this neighborhood."

Wilson started to feel the anger boiling inside him. Who did Mr. McConnell think he was? He was smiling at Wilson like Wilson didn't know anything about the plans he had with his mother, things that would destroy their family forever.

"How's that eye feeling?" Richard asked as he walked to the edge of the lawn. Wilson couldn't control his anger anymore.

"Richard, have you ever been inside our house?" Wilson asked. There was no time for niceties with this homewrecker. The man looked curiously at Wilson.

"Mr. McConnell is fine. Thank you."

Wilson ignored the correction and repeated the question.

"Have you been to our house, *Richard*?"

Mr. McConnell looked startled, and after seeing the seriousness in Wilson's face, the man was genuinely confused.

"What do you mean?"

"Have you visited our house?"

The man paused before answering.

"You know what? I think I went into that house when they were building it a few years back. Beautiful architecture. I wish I would've chosen that spot before your parents snatched it off the market."

"That's not what I mean. Have you been in the house recently?"

"Hey, Wilson. I don't know what..."

"You've been in our house. I know you have."

"I think you're confused. Maybe you should..."

"You've visited several times when my Dad was working. You went in to visit my mother and the two of you..."

Richard's face turned bright red. Wilson could tell he made the man angry.

"Look! Is this a joke or something? You'd better get out of here before I..."

At that moment, the man's front door opened. A woman with large rollers in her hair stuck her head out the door and yelled.

"Richard! Your boss is on the phone!"

"Okay, I'll be right in."

The man turned back to Wilson and whispered.

"Look. I understand you haven't been feeling well lately, but that's no reason to go around insinuating things. Go home, Wilson. Go home before I call your folks."

But the man's words held no power with Wilson. The sound of Richard's voice made Wilson angrier.

"Call them. In fact, why don't you call my dad? Tell him what I said. You think I don't know what you're doing with my mom?" Wilson asked. The man looked nervously at his front door to see if his wife had heard the words. When he was sure she wasn't there, he charged across his lawn towards Wilson.

"Hey! You shut your dirty mouth!" he screamed.

"I know about everything! I know about the visits to our house while my dad was working. I know about the trip you're planning to London. I know it all!"

"How did you know...I never told anyone..."

"Leave my mom alone!"

"Look, you little shit! Get the hell out of here before I kick your ass!"

But Wilson didn't budge. Instead, he did something so unexpected that he surprised himself. With his two fingers, he tapped gently on the eyelid of his white eye. Suddenly, the whole neighborhood was dark.

"What's happening?" Mr. McConnell asked as he fell backward onto the lawn. "What's going on?"

Wilson moved closer. Richard lay shivering in fear on the grass, terrified as the child approached him.

"You stay away from my mother," Wilson growled, his voice a hissing echo inside the darkness. As he lay in the grass, Richard felt the ground begin to shake. Terrified, he looked at Wilson with wide eyes.

"What are you?" he asked. Mr. McConnell attempted to stand but fell to the ground as the earth shook everything around them. Soon car alarms up and down the street began blaring. A terrifying scream came from within Mr. McConnell's house.

"Becky!" yelled Mr. McConnell. The screams belonged to his wife.

"Richard! Help!" the woman yelled as the sounds of crashing dishes came from inside the house.

"Please! Tell me what you want!"

"Leave my family alone!"

"Okay! Okay! Please! Just stop!"

Suddenly the ground stopped shaking. A freezing burst of wind blew into Richard's face that took his breath away. He covered his head and curled up into a ball on the lawn.

"What do you want?" he yelled as he lay cowering. There was no response. Cautiously, Richard sat up and looked around.

As soon as he looked at the child, Wilson wiped his fingers across his eyelid again. This time after doing so, he aimed both his fingers at the man. Richard started trembling uncontrollably. As if a giant invisible monster had grabbed him, his body rose in the air with both his arms extended.

"Please! Stop!" Richard screamed. Wilson ripped the man's leg from his body. Then his arm. Then his other leg. Blood sprayed all over the lawn.

"Aaaaagh..." the man cried. His face became as white as a bedsheet, and his eyes rolled back in his head. He began having a seizure as the blood drained from his body.

After a few moments, Wilson became aware of what was occurring. His eyes blinked, and he looked around.

"No!" he yelled.

There was a loud sound, like lightning striking the whole neighborhood at once. The light temporarily blinded Wilson, and he closed his eyes. When he opened them again, Richard was lying on his lawn whole. The man stood to his feet and stumbled back towards the house.

"Okay. You win! I won't do it anymore. I swear."

As soon as Mr. McConnell opened the front door to his house, Wilson heard his wife.

"What's going on? Was that an earthquake?"

Wilson smiled and started walking back towards his house. His family was safe – for now.

8

Dumb Little Brothers

Wilson climbed into bed and stared at the ceiling. He couldn't help thinking about his run-in with Richard. Had it been real, or was it a hallucination? If it was real, how did he know how to access the power? What other abilities did he possess? Frustrated with all the questions in his head, Wilson turned to his brother. Michael was sleeping on the bed beside him.

"Mike!" he whispered. "Mike! You awake?"

His brother stirred and turned over to face Wilson.

"What? I was sleeping."

"Something's happening with my eye."

Michael sat up in bed.

"You want me to go get mom?"

"No. It's nothing like that."

"What's the problem?"

"I'm seeing things now."

"Seeing things like what?"

"Like I imagine things."

"Did you tell mom and dad?"

"No. Mom and Dad wouldn't understand."

"I think you should. What if you have an accident?"

"I thought about that."

"Well?"

"I only see things when I touch my eye."

Michael climbed out of bed and went over to sit on the edge of Wilson's bed.

"Go ahead. Touch it."

"Are you crazy? No way!"

"Why not?"

"Because the things I see are scary."

"Scary how?"

"Today, I saw Mr. McConnell down the street."

"And?"

"And I pulled off his arms and legs."

Michael moved closer.

"You did? Cool!"

"No, it wasn't cool. I was scared as hell. I can't get that image out of my head."

"Wait. How did you pull off Mr. McConnell's arms and legs? Did you change into a superhero? Did you transform into a man with muscles? How did you do it?"

Wilson looked at his brother and laid back down on his bed. It was a bad idea to confide in his brother.

"Never mind. Go to bed."

"No, dude. You have to spill your guts on this one. How did it happen?"

"Goodnight, Mike."

Reluctantly, Michael went back to his bed and climbed in.

"Fuck you. Don't wake me up again," Michael said before turning away from Wilson.

"Fuck you too," Wilson replied.

After a few moments, he called out to his brother again.

"Hey, Mike?"

"Yeah."

"Don't tell."

"Okay."

Seconds later, both the boys fell asleep.

9

The Argument

At breakfast, Wilson could tell that things weren't right between his parents. They weren't speaking to each other and only answered Wilson and Michael in simple yes or no answers. At lunch, things escalated even further when Wilson's father tried to grab a glass from the cupboard while their mother stood in front of it. After retrieving the cup and walking away, Wilson's mom exploded.

"The phrase is *excuse me*!" she yelled before slamming her pot in the sink. "Fucking jackass!"

Wilson and Michael went about their day trying to ignore the tension, but soon it became too much to ignore. While Michael and Wilson watched tv in the den, their mother and father confronted one another in the kitchen. Both the children walked to the living room and sat on the couch, pretending to read books while listening to the war taking place in the other room.

"I don't care! I'm not driving them there!"

"We have to. I told mom we were arriving tomorrow."

"Well, there you go! You're always acting like a momma's boy! Anything to make her happy! No Christmases. No Thanksgivings! You always give in to whatever she wants. *Let the boys stay here every summer. Okay, mom. Don't cut the boys' hair. Okay, mom.* You have our sons walking around here with hair longer than mine. I mean, fuck! Get some guts!"

"It's part of our heritage, Julia. And don't start with the Thanksgiving complaints. You know good and damned well why we don't celebrate that holiday in our family."

"Oh yeah. I forgot. The sensitive Native Americans. What about my culture, huh? Do you expect me to always give in to what your mom wants? Do you ever think about how our sons will be outcasts in college? What are they supposed to tell their friends when everyone goes home for the holidays?"

"Oh, here we go—the white girl with all the culture. Please enlighten me. Tell me about all the cultural events our sons are missing. Halloween? Columbus Day? Fuck that!"

"What are they supposed to tell their friends at college? Huh? What are they supposed to say when one of them brings a girl home from school? *Do you boys have girlfriends? Sure, you can bring them home to meet us. Just make sure it's not on a holiday that pisses us off.* What are we supposed to say about that, genius?"

"First of all, the boys are not going to college for years. Stop being dramatic. And secondly, what's wrong with telling them the truth about those holidays? They're bullshit holidays meant to make Americans feel good about the slaughtering of our people."

"Fuck you, Dustin. If you want to take them there, you go alone! Something is at your mom's house that's making Wilson sick. I won't help you send him to his death."

"You think I'm a fool, don't you?"

"What do you mean?"

"You think I don't know the real reason you want to stay at home?"

Julia paused before she continued speaking.

"Our son is changing into a freak!"

"Lower your voice. Wilson will hear you."

"You think he doesn't know how strange he looks? Everybody in the neighborhood talks about this whole house like we're from Mars."

"Your exploits aren't helping."

"I haven't done anything wrong that you didn't deserve."

"Oh, now I deserve it?"

"I guess your secretary calling you all hours of the day is normal."

"For my job, it is. I have never cheated on you, and I never will. Can you say the same?"

"Look! I'm not going. If you want to take the boys there, you go alone! Something is at your mom's house that's making Wilson sick. I won't help you send him to his death."

"Fuck it. We'll go alone."

Wilson's father stormed out of the kitchen. After realizing his sons had heard the whole conversation, his face turned red with shame.

"Boys."

Michael stood and walked out the front door to the porch. After his dad retreated to his bedroom, Wilson joined his brother.

10

Going Home

Wilson laid his head on the car window and watched as the cars zoomed by. They were only an hour into their long road trip, and his brother Michael had already fallen asleep. Wilson's mom had decided to stay home. For some reason, she had become depressed after the argument with Wilson's father and didn't come out of the bedroom. Aside from wondering what his mother was up to, Wilson wasn't bothered. He was happy his mom didn't come. All she would've done was to complain and fight with his dad. Having a guys-only trip would give his mom time to think about her infidelity.

"You boys okay back there?" asked Dustin. Michael was almost asleep, so Wilson was the only one to respond.

"Yeah, Dad. We're okay."

Dustin looked in the rearview mirror at his son.

"Hey...about yesterday..."

Wilson tried to change the subject.

"Are you going to be staying at Grandma's with us for a day or two?"

Dustin smiled.

"Don't do that, son. Now, about yesterday's fight. I didn't realize you guys were there listening. If I had known, we would've done our little dance in the bedroom."

"It's okay, Dad. Really."

"No. It's not okay. Your mom didn't mean what she said about you being a freak."

"Yes, she did. But that's just how she is. But what she said was true. People do talk about me."

"How are you dealing with that? The added attention."

"It's weird because I feel as normal as I ever did. It's just…"

"What?"

"I see things sometimes."

"You do? Like what?"

"I don't know. It's just that things are different."

Dustin looked at his son in the mirror.

"Talk to Grandma Noya about it. She's great with listening."

"I know."

Wilson was quiet for a moment, and then he spoke.

"Are you and mom getting a divorce?"

"No. I don't think so. People who are married for a long amount of time go through their ups and downs. Right now, your mother and I are at the down point of our relationship."

"But Mr. McConnell…"

Dustin's eyes widened.

"How do you know his name?"

"Nobody told me. I just guessed."

"Has he been to the house?"

"No. At least not while we were there."

"Look. No matter what happens between you and your mom, just know that we both love you and your brother. And nothing will ever change that. Okay?"

"Okay, Dad."

Wilson laid his head back on the seat. If his Dad and Mom did get divorced, he knew which parent he would choose. Wilson closed his eyes. After a while, he fell asleep.

11

Buffalo Dreams

Wilson was walking through a lush green field, enjoying the warm sunshine on his face. He took a deep breath and exhaled. The fragrance of fresh flowers filled the air. As Wilson walked through the field, he could see bumblebees landing on the large flowers all around him.

"Wilson!" a voice rang out from behind him. The boy turned to look back. He could see a small house far away.

"Wilson! Come back!" the voice yelled again.

Wilson recognized the voice. It was his brother Michael.

"What do you want?" he yelled. There was no response.

"What is it?" Wilson yelled once more. Suddenly Michael ran down from the porch and started frantically waving his hands.

"What?"

Wilson turned away from his brother and looked up into the sky. He saw a large black cloud in the distance, absorbing smaller clouds near it and gaining strength. He turned back to the house and screamed at his brother.

"Is that it? Is that what you're screaming about?" he asked. But he could no longer see Michael's face. The only thing remaining was a tall, thin shadow. Wilson turned to look at the cloud again. It was much bigger than before. There was a strange smell in the air that he didn't recognize.

"I'd better head back," he exclaimed. He turned around and stopped. The house was gone.

"Michael! Where are you?" Wilson yelled across the field. But his brother couldn't be found. Wilson started walking in the direction he had last seen his brother when a burst of wind pushed against his back, knocking him to the ground. Wilson jumped to his feet and turned around. The storm cloud looked menacing now, lights flashing inside it as it moved closer. A huge lightning bolt reached out from the cloud and struck a tree in the distance. Sparks flew into the air, and the tree burst into flames. Wilson was terrified. He was all alone with no place to go. He spun around, looking in all directions for shelter.

"Hey! Michael!" he yelled again. "Where are you?"

The only response was the deep rumble of thunder pushing across the field. Wilson's heart pounded as he looked up at the black cloud above him. Although he wasn't afraid, he could feel that something was about to happen. Wilson felt the electricity of the storm calling out to him, pulling at him as it drew closer. Just as he was about to turn around to try to make a run for it, the cloud sent three massive bolts of electricity into the ground, dazzling the field in white light. Wilson took off running, but it was too late. Large raindrops dropped from the sky, drenching everything around him. The rain was so heavy that it blocked his vision. Soon the rain became so powerful that he couldn't run, and all Wilson could do was walk through the field. After a while, he was surrounded by so much water that each step felt like wading through a pond. After a while, his legs felt like he had weights attached to them. Wilson stopped walking and stood looking into the darkness of the rain, trying to locate something that would give him respite from the deluge.

That's when he spotted it.

Something was moving across the field toward him. Unsure of what it was, Wilson wiped at his eyes and peered into the rain. The large brown mass seemed to cover half of the field. Water splashed all around it as it drew closer.

"What is that?" Wilson yelled into the rain.

Suddenly, his brother Michael was beside him.

"She told me they would come for you," said Michael.

"Why did she tell you that?" asked Wilson.

Michael looked confused. As he turned to walk away, Wilson grabbed him by the arm.

"Why did she tell you that?" he repeated. Confused, Michael looked away.

"Who?"

"You know."

"Who, Michael?"

Wilson's brother pointed into the rain.

"They're here."

The brown mass was much closer now, and Wilson began to shake. It was a gigantic herd of buffalo. The fantastic beasts blew puffs of steam from the nostrils as they galloped towards the two boys. The ground shook as the animals' powerful legs pounded into the rain puddles in the field. As the animals drew closer, Wilson closed his eyes and prepared for impact.

But there was none.

After a few seconds, he opened his eyes to find that the rain was gone. Instead of puddles, he was standing in a field bathed in sunshine. Two large buffaloes stood in front of him, breathing heavily. The larger of the two animals then nudged gently at Wilson's hand.

"Hello," said Wilson as he rubbed the animal's head. Suddenly the beast turned to Wilson and let out a loud bellow. The boy stumbled back and fell to the ground. When he looked up, someone was standing above him – a woman. Wilson couldn't see her face because it was in shadow.

"Who...who are you?"

"Get up."

The woman extended her hand to lift Wilson from the ground. When Wilson stood up, the woman was gone.

"Prepare yourself. It's your turn," a voice whispered across the field. Suddenly the area burst into flames, and Wilson screamed out in pain. His body was on fire.

12

The House

"Wake up, boy."

Wilson woke up and looked around the car. His Grandmother smiled at him.

"Time to get your bags," she said as she leaned into the car and rubbed his head. Wilson wiped the saliva from his mouth and opened the car door.

"Be careful. Let your brother sleep a little more," Wilson's father yelled from the opposite side of the car. Wilson looked over at his brother sleeping in the back seat.

"I should wake him up," he whispered. After all, Wilson would be the one sweating through chores while his brother played video games. Tempted to wake up his little brother rudely as he continued sleeping in the car, Wilson decided against it and got his bags from the trunk. As soon as he started carrying the bags to the house, his grandmother stopped him.

"What are you doing?"

"Taking my bags to the house."

"No. You and Michael are going to stay in Nana Ama's house."

Wilson dropped his bags on the lawn.

"What?"

Grandma Noya started smiling while Wilson's father burst into laughter.

"You're joking, right?"

The smile disappeared from the old woman's face.

"No. I'm not joking. It's time for you boys to learn how to take care of yourselves."

"But…"

"Why do you think I was making you do all those chores? It was to teach you how to be independent."

Wilson nervously stared at the old house across the street.

"Couldn't you teach us another way? Nana Ama died in that house."

A frown came over the woman's face, and she lowered her head.

"I know, Mom," whispered Wilson's father. He tapped her gently on the arm as she moved towards the bags.

"Your Nana will be happy to see you," said Grandma Noya.

Wilson shot a scared look at his dad.

"Her ghost?"

"If you want to use those words."

"I'm afraid of ghosts."

Wilson was lying. Ever since he discovered his new powers, there was truly little that made him afraid. Still, the possibility of a run-in with his Great Grandmother's spirit made him nervous.

Grandma Noya lifted the bag and carried it onto the porch. Wilson's dad walked over to him and slapped him on the back.

"Is that what makes you afraid? Ghosts?"

"I mean…yeah. Aren't you?"

"What do you think happens when you die?"

"I don't know."

"I'll be sure to tell your Grandmother to explain life and death to you. She explained it to me when I was your age. It's cool."

"But…the house. I don't want to stay there."

"Michael will be with you. It'll be an adventure."

Michael walked up behind Wilson and Dustin as they talked.

"What's going on?"

"You and your brother will be staying in Nana Ama's house on this visit."

"Really? Alone?"

"Your Grandmother will be staying with you for a night or two. But mostly, it'll be just you and Wilson."

The boy took the news much differently than Wilson.

"Cool! That's awesome!"

He ran into the house and left his father and brother in the yard.

"Don't worry. You and your brother will probably like the freedom."

"I don't think so."

"You do realize it's not permanently dark in that house, right? You guys get to be men away from your parents. Mom will bring you food and stay out of your way. I did it when I was a kid."

"You did?"

"Sure. Your grandmother isn't a fool. I learned how to be a man in that house."

"Was Nana Ama there with you?"

"Sure, she was—just me and her. We sat up talking and joking all night. It was fun."

"You joked with Nana Ama? I never saw her smile."

"That was years ago when I was a kid. She became more serious over time. I guess old age changed her a bit. I know she's gone now, but you don't need to fear her absence. If anything, you should feel safe. She loved all of us and would never let anything bad happen. Trust me. Nana Ama's spirit loves you."

As the two walked into the house, Wilson looked nervously at his father. He had his doubts.

Wilson, Michael, and Grandma Noya walked to the edge of the driveway and watched until Dustin's car disappeared in the morning sun. Although his father had stayed the night with them, Wilson wished his Dad had stayed longer. He knew his father's heart would break as soon as he returned home to find Wilson's mother gone.

"Cheer up, boys," said Grandma Noya. "Today is the day."

"For what?" asked Michael.

"Today is the day you learn about the elders," she replied.

Wilson was confused.

"You mean Nana Ama?"

"Yes, she's a large part of that lesson. But you can't learn about your Nana without knowing Wilson Jones. Their spirits are one."

"I thought you told us to never speak of Great Grandfather Wilson."

"You were too young at the time. But now things have changed. You are older. Wiser. It is time."

Grandma Noya walked back towards the house.

"We'll eat a good breakfast before we start our journey."

Wilson and Michael looked at one another.

"Journey?" asked Wilson.

"Yes. Today we visit your Great Grandfather."

13

The History Lesson

After breakfast, Grandma Noya washed the dishes and changed from her everyday skirt into some jeans and a large sunhat. After the boys changed from shorts into jeans, they marveled at their grandmother's appearance. They'd become accustomed to seeing her dressed in her usual bland "Grandmother" attire. It never occurred to them that she was more than they knew.

"Okay. Are you boys ready?" she asked as she walked down the steps of the front porch.

"Yes," the boys replied while following her.

"You boys are going to have to keep up. The weeds are thick, and the forest is dark. Wilson, be sure to hold Michael's hand."

As the group neared the edge of the front yard, Grandma Noya made a turn to go around the house. Wilson spoke up.

"I thought we were going to Nana Ama's house."

"No. We'll go there tonight. But today we need to visit your Great Grandfather's house. He stays in the forest behind our house."

As the group pushed through the weeds past Grandma Noya's pigpen, all the pigs moved to the trough expecting food. The stench of mud, spoiled food, and pig excrement began choking the boys, and they both pinched their noses.

"Shoooo..." Grandma Noya said in a high voice to calm the pigs. As the group moved past the pigpen, the weeds started to become taller.

Grandma Noya noticed a group of blackbirds circling up above and swung her arms in the air to scare them away.

"They think I'm bringing food to the pigs. No food today."

Grandma Noya stepped through the weeds like she was a giant. Every step she took, Wilson and Michael had to take two to keep up with her. It wasn't long before the boys lost sight of her. They could hear her pushing steadily through the weeds, but they could no longer see her. After a while, they yelled out to her.

"Grandma! Grandma! Slow down!"

Still, they couldn't see her.

"Where did she go?" asked Michael, clinging to his brother's hand. Wilson yelled again.

"Grandma! Hey!"

Just as they pushed through the next set of tall weeds, Wilson ran into his grandmother's stomach, and both boys tumbled to the ground.

"City kids," she grumbled. "I'll move a little slower, but you need to keep up. We're almost in the forest."

The group walked on for a few steps more and stopped. Wilson and Michael wiped the sweat from the brows and froze. The edge of the forest looked like a massive fortress of trees, vines, and bushes climbing up into the sky.

"Whoa," exclaimed Michael. "We're going in there?"

Grandma Noya walked to an opening beside a large tree.

"This way. Keep up."

Just as Wilson took the first step, a large snake slid across his path.

"Snake! Snake!" he yelled and pulled his brother back. Michael peered from behind his brother at the creature.

"It's huge!" he exclaimed.

Grandma Noya stepped out from the forest and walked over to the snake. Calmly, she lifted the creature and tossed him into the weeds. The boys looked at their Grandmother in astonishment.

"Why are you afraid? There is too much of the city in you. Now let's go."

As soon as he entered the forest, Wilson took a deep breath. It was as if he walked into another world. All the sounds he'd heard in the weeds disappeared. Stepping inside the forest was like roaming inside a large empty container of milk. Other than the occasional hoot from an owl, there was nothing. It was as if something had swallowed all the sound of the world. The forest floor had thousands of black pine needles. The trees' bark had been singed and looked as if someone dipped them in ink.

"Was there a fire here?" asked Wilson. His Grandmother turned to look at him before continuing to walk into the darkness.

"Yes. We burn the forest every two years to prevent forest fires."

"Who? You and Uncle Charlie?"

"Me, your uncle, and a few neighbors from town. It's better than having lightning strike a tree and sparking a fire."

Michael stopped walking and looked around.

"You hear that, Wilson?" he asked. Wilson listened.

"Crickets," he responded. "I never heard them in the middle of the day."

Grandma Noya chimed in.

"Do you think life stops when the sun sets? No. Life must continue."

"How much longer do we need to walk?" complained Michael. Grandma Noya stopped.

"Wilson, how much do you know about your Great Grandfather?"

"Not much because you told us not to talk about him."

Grandma Noya started walking again.

"Your Great Grandfather's family were freed slaves turned sharecroppers. Do you boys know what a sharecropper is?"

"No," the two boys responded.

"Well, a long time ago, America allowed slavery. Michael, you know what slavery is, right?"

"I think so."

This time Wilson spoke up.

"We studied it in social studies. It's when someone takes away your freedom and forces you to work for them."

"That's right. Now, when slavery ended, sharecropping was a way for landowners to continue to have their fields worked. Instead of slaves, they allowed workers to live on the land and split a portion of the owner's wages. Understand?"

"Like partners, right?"

"Yes and no. In theory, it was supposed to be like that. But the reality of the arrangement was much different. Outlawing slavery didn't mean that everyone immediately stopped practicing oppression. There were a lot of broken promises, abuse, and exploitation. For years, the Jones family worked on two plantations: the Smith Plantation and the Pervis Plantation. Things were okay until a worker at the Smith Plantation was beaten to death by the owner over a bad tobacco crop. Paul, your Great Grandfather Wilson's father, decided to leave and work exclusively at the Pervis Plantation. Mr. Pervis was a friendly owner, but more importantly, he was fair to the six families that lived on his property. And for Paul, fairness was a rare thing in the South. The pay was above average, and the owner didn't interfere too much in the workers' daily lives. It was a fairly good set up for Wilson and his family. They stayed and tried to make a life for themselves."

Grandma Noya stopped talking. The group arrived in a grassy clearing full of sunshine and birds.

"We can rest here for a bit."

Grateful for the rest, both boys flopped down on the grass and wiped the sweat from their brows. Grandma Noya took a sip from her canteen and passed it to her grandsons. They each drank from the canteen as if they hadn't had water in days.

"You boys need to get more exercise. Too many video games."

At that moment, a large brown deer entered the clearing and stared at the group resting on the grass.

"Wow. A deer!" exclaimed Michael.

"Quiet child," whispered Grandma Noya. "She's not alone."

Seconds later, a spotted fawn emerged from the dark forest. The small animal looked at the group curiously before following its mother into the woods. Grandma Noya continued her story.

"Anyway, like I was saying, your Great Grandfather Wilson and his family spent many years at the Pervis Plantation. But one day, Mr. Pervis disappeared. An evil man named Mr. Green took his place and started bossing the workers around. He set up men with guns around the property's perimeter and held the workers against their will. Anyone attempting to leave was taken to the center of the property and killed for all to witness. He took away the free time that the workers had for their families and made them work unreasonable hours. Mr. Green treated families like animals."

Grandma Noya stood and slung the canteen onto her shoulder.

"Okay, boys. Only a little further to go."

Grandma Noya led the boys through the forest for a half mile before they emerged in a field. Wilson stopped and looked around. He had seen the area before. Perched sitting at the far end of the field was an old house.

"I've seen this place," whispered Wilson. Grandma Noya nodded towards the house. "Your Great Grandfather is buried behind that house."

As the three walked across the field, Grandma Noya continued her story.

"One day, Paul was in the fields cutting tobacco when he came upon the first owner's body. Mr. Pervis had been shot and buried in a shallow grave amongst the tobacco. Paul went back to the families and told everyone what he had found. Word got back to Mr. Green, and he beat Paul and dropped him in an old dry well in his backyard. Mr. Green kept him there for weeks. He threw rotten food down to him and forced him to eat it. He made the guards take turns urinating on him. They threw rocks at him and cursed him."

"When they finally pulled Paul out of the hole, he had so many maggots on him that the worms seemed to be a part of his skin. But the abuse didn't stop there. Mr. Green assaulted the Jones family by beating your Great Grandfather and his mother with whips in front of the community."

Finally, the group arrived in front of the house. Michael moved close to his grandmother and stared at the home.

"That house is spooky," he whispered.

"You need to be strong," she replied. "The only spirits here are of your family. Your blood. There's nothing to be afraid of on this land."

Grandma Noya grabbed Michael's hand and began walking around the side of the house to the backyard. Michael looked back at his brother.

"Come on, Wilson," Michael yelled. "Why are you just standing there?"

But Wilson was frozen in fear. Standing on the front porch was a ghost, a shirtless black man covered in blood. His face was grotesque, swollen with deep gashes on his forehead. One of his eyes was missing, the eye socket teaming with thick white maggots.

Grandma Noya looked back at Wilson and paused. After a few seconds, she pulled Michael ahead.

"Don't worry about your brother. He has to take his path for himself," she said.

As the two disappeared around the house's corner, Wilson remained standing in front of the house, unable to move. Slowly, the ghost descended the stairs and began walking to him.

"Protect the family..." the ghost whispered.

Wilson took a step back. Still, the ghost continued forward.

"He approaches. The Evil One. You must protect the family."

Wilson turned around to run across the field but stopped in his tracks. There were dozens of ghosts standing in front of him, all of them with their hands outstretched.

"Protect your family. He approaches," they all said. Wilson's heart was pounding. There were children, women, and men. Young and old. All of them wearing the stench of death, their flesh gray and decaying.

"Grandma!" yelled Wilson. But she didn't hear him. Suddenly, Wilson felt a tugging on his arm. He looked down to see a Native American little girl pulling on his arm.

"Agowatiha!" she whispered. "Seeeeee...."

Suddenly Wilson was surrounded by darkness. After a few moments, his eyes adjusted to the light. He was at the bottom of a deep hole. The dull glow of the moon was the only light he had to see.

"Grandma! Michael!" he yelled. "Help! I'm trapped."

Wilson heard whispering above him. There was shuffling and more whispering.

"Hey! Is anybody up there?"

A loud evil laugh rang out. Suddenly a white man's face appeared over the hole.

"Are you hungry, boy?"

"Please, can you help me get out of here?" pleaded Wilson.

The man ignored him.

"Too bad, you missed supper. No worries. I saved some vittles for you."

Suddenly Wilson's body was drenched in a milky substance that smelled like vomit. He looked on the ground around him and saw chicken bones, rotting meat, and other spoiled food items all around him. Vomit shot out of Wilson's mouth, and he fell back against the wall of the well.

"Hahahaha...how do you like your dinner?" laughed the voice from above.

"Fuck you!" Wilson cursed as he brushed the slop out of his hair. The man above the well continued laughing and then stopped. Wilson moved close to the wall and reached up for a hold of something to climb out. As soon as he placed his hand on the concrete, he felt something cold crawling on his skin. He held up his hand for inspection and saw a large maggot crawling up his arm.

"Aaaaaahhh!"

Wilson screamed and fell on his back in the rotten food. Suddenly maggots were all over his body. As he tried to brush them off, more and more appeared. Soon he couldn't move his body anymore. The rotten food became a deep pool of filth pulling on his body like a suction. The maggots were overwhelming. One by one, he felt the creatures crawl up his neck, to his face, and into his eye. Wilson felt one of the insects on his eyelid. When it touched his eyeball, a jolt of pain shot through Wilson's head, and he saw a blinding light.

When Wilson could see again, he was standing in front of the house again. Grandma Noya and Michael came walking around the corner of the house hand in hand.

"Hey, Wilson. Aren't you going to see our Great Grandfather's grave?" asked Michael. Wilson turned away from him and started walking back towards the forest.

"I saw Great Grandfather Wilson's grave already. Are we ready to go home now?"

Sensing Wilson's fear, Grandma Noya smiled and took Michael's hand.

"Let's go. We'll come back some other time."

As the trio started walking back home through the forest, Wilson peppered Grandma Noya with questions.

"Did Paul escape the hole?"

"Eventually, they let him out. But by then, he was too injured to work. He went blind in one of his eyes because it got infected from dozens of insect bites. They took him into the forest and left him to die. But he didn't."

"What happened?"

"After they left Paul to die, two Cherokee hunters came along and found him. They took him back to their tribe. After explaining to their leader about the slave master, the leader let Paul stay. It turns out Mr.

Green had murdered men from their tribe, and they were hunting him as well. The tribe nursed Paul back to health."

"Really? That was nice."

"Paul convinced the Cherokee tribe to help him launch an assault on Mr. Green and his men. One night they invaded the community. When it was over, Mr. Green was captured and brought before Paul for judgment. Paul killed Mr. Green. Paul divided the land with the tribe, and he lived on the small plot we visited until he died."

"But how did Great Grandpa Wilson meet Nana Ama?"

"She was the person who helped care for Paul. Years after the battle, she continued to take care of him. That is when she met Wilson. Although they were barely ten years old, they became close. When they were old enough, and they had gotten the blessing of the elders, they were married."

Grandma Noya stopped.

"Michael, do you want to ride on my back?"

She noticed that the boy was silent during the conversation. Fatigue was weighing heavily on his eyelids.

"No, Grandma. I'm fine."

Wilson looked at his little brother and stuck out his tongue. Michael straightened his back and continued marching through the dark forest. They continued marching on for thirty more minutes until they finally exited the woods at the end of Grandma Noya's pigpen.

14

At the Gate of Evil

Grandma Noya moved a second rocking chair in front of the large bay window in the bedroom. Next, she brought in a lamp from the living room and placed it on the small table next to the chairs.

"I put a low-watt bulb in here so you boys can leave this on all night. You know, in case you get scared," she said.

"Scared? I'm not scared," piped Michael.

"Me either," replied Wilson. Grandma Noya looked at both the boys and winked.

"I know you're not."

After sitting in the kitchen and finishing off a plate of chocolate chip cookies, the two boys showered and brushed their teeth. When they went into the bedroom, Grandma Noya had two sleeping bags next to the bed.

"I'll sleep on the bed tonight. You guys will be roughing it in those sleeping bags," she said.

"Cool!" replied Michael. He quickly unzipped his sleeping bag and climbed in. Wilson walked over to the rocking chairs sitting in front of the window.

"I'm not sleepy," he said. He sat down in one of the rocking chairs and looked out past the backyard towards the edge of the forest. He didn't know why, but it felt like something was out there. Seeing Wilson staring into the woods, Grandma Noya walked over and sat in the chair beside his.

"What's troubling you, child?"

"I don't know. Maybe it's my eye."

Grandma Noya started rocking slowly in her chair.

"Michael. Come over here and sit with us."

The small boy unzipped his sleeping bag and went over to the chairs. Grandma Noya lifted him on her lap.

"Wilson. About your eye, have you noticed anything special about it?"

Wilson sat up in his chair.

"You mean the color?"

The old woman gave Wilson a stern look. Sensing Grandmother Noya could see through his lies, Wilson responded again.

"The visions."

"Your eye is a special trait in our family. It is not unique to you. Part of its power comes from the slaves. You know, your Great Grandfather's part of the family."

Michael spoke up.

"Nana Ama had it?"

Grandma Noya smiled and kissed the boy on the cheek.

"Eventually, yes, she did."

She lifted Michael off her lap.

"Sit with your brother."

As soon as the child climbed into the chair, Grandma Noya stood and walked out of the room. Seconds later, she returned with a large white photo album.

"There have been four people in our family to have the gift."

Grandma Noya flipped through the album showing photos of various family members with varying eye colors.

"My father was the first that I knew to get this power: your Great Grandfather, Wilson Jones. Nana Ama told me that she knew of two people in his family that had the gift. All of them experienced the same thing. The changing eye color, the visions…"

"Where did it come from?"

"Nobody knows for sure. My father's family were Africans brought to this country against their will. We thought the eye color and the visions were those of my father's tribe in Africa. But I never knew my Father's parents so I couldn't find out. They died long before I was born – before my father realized he had powers."

"Powers?" asked the two boys in unison.

"Yes."

Grandma Noya stood up and looked out the window.

"Come here, boys."

Both Wilson and Michael stood and walked closer to the window.

"Look out into the darkness. There is a faint light out where the trees are. Do you see it?"

The two boys stared out into the darkness.

"I see it," said Michael.

"Yes, I see it!" replied Wilson. "What is it?"

"That place is where the earth ends, and the Underworld begins. There are angry evil spirits there. They are constantly trying to escape the Underworld. Our backyard stands between the gates of hell and the rest of the world. Sometimes the creatures crawl up from the forest and try to escape, but they can't get out. They don't have enough strength to enter our world. As soon as the first rays of daylight appear, their souls return to the forest."

"Who calls them? The Devil?"

"No one knows for sure who he is, but sometimes I think it's Mr. Green. We simply call him the *Evil One*. He traps lost spirits and tries to keep them for his own."

"Mr. Green? How is that possible? How long has that place been there? Where did it come from?"

"I'm going to tell you about the history of this place. Okay? Pay attention."

The children sat up and listened to Grandma Noya.

"That evil place has been there for many years, but your Great Grandfather Wilson discovered what the place was."

"He did? How?"

"He had a vision come to him through his eye."

"What did he see in the vision?"

"The vision showed him how the forest became a gateway to the underworld. It showed him the history of the forest. Do you remember what I told you about Mr. Green?"

"Yes. I remember. Mr. Green is the man that tortured our Great Grandfather."

"Yes, that's him. The evil of that man runs deep in this land. He's the person that originally owned this property as well as mine across the street. Mr. Green was the kind of man most wealthy men are; careless with their money, arrogant, evil, and vindictive. He and Mr. Pervis used to be friends. Do you remember who Mr. Pervis was?"

"He was the original landowner that worked with the sharecroppers," replied Michael. Grandma Noya smiled.

"Good memory, Michael. Mr. Pervis and Mr. Green were friends. One night they were playing cards, and Mr. Green lost the property to Mr. Pervis in a card game."

"He did?"

"That's the day they stopped being friends. Mr. Pervis took his land and started growing crops on it. He hired several sharecropping families and started harvesting his crops for a profit. Meanwhile, Mr. Green wallowed in hatred against Mr. Pervis. He continuously thought of ways to kill him to take back the land he felt was rightfully his. It wasn't long until he started trying to make his murderous fantasies a reality. He went into the forest and began building machines to help him fulfill his bloodlust. That is when the killing began."

Grandma Noya stood and looked out into the dark forest.

"There's a mass grave in that forest where Mr. Green murdered thousands of men, women, and children. Mr. Green's forest was a place where like-minded evil men who didn't believe in abolishing slavery would congregate to play with the souls of the innocents to their hearts' content. Men traveled from all over the country to participate in the pain. Thousands of them traveled for miles with their cargo of "useless slaves" and "criminals" to see Mr. Green's torture machines bend bones and break spirits. Mr. Green was a man that took great pleasure in the suffering of others. Any person that he took to that forest endured torture beyond comprehension. He wasn't satisfied unless he heard men beg for their lives. The cries of his victims as he ran them through his torture machines made him want more pain. He craved more cruelty. He did sadistic things to the corpses, things that were beyond evil. But eventually, he became unable to satisfy his thirst for death and turned to hell for inspiration. Day after day, he called out to the underworld to take his soul, but they didn't answer. He cut himself and spilled his blood in hopes that the Underworld would reward him for his suffering. But nothing happened. It wasn't long before he turned his evil gaze on children. He kidnapped several children from a Cherokee tribe and ran them through his torture machines. After discovering what he'd done, Cherokees from other states rode in to track him down. Eventually, your Great Grandfather killed Mr. Green. That is the moment the Underworld took his soul."

"What happened after that?"

"The place was quiet for a while until strange things started happening. Some hunters went into the forest and never returned. There used to be a huge herd of buffalo roaming this property. They were big, beautiful creatures. One day they were here, and the next, they were gone. My father saw them walking towards the forest one day, and he never saw them again. After that, the whispers started. People around town started saying that an evil spirit cursed the land. The birds left. And then we started seeing spirits."

"Spirits?"

"I think you kids call them ghosts. Your Great Grandfather saw the first ghost. One evening he was walking on the property when he saw the ghost of a little Cherokee child roaming the edge of the forest. She only said a few words to my father."

"What did she say?"

"She said the Evil One told her to murder her tribe."

"What tribe? The Cherokees?"

"Yes."

The two boys stared at their Grandma in fear. The old woman continued to speak.

"The little girl terrified your Great Grandfather so much that he went to the Cherokee tribe and told them what he saw. The leader became angry. He blamed my father for bringing their tribe into the Underworld's sight with Mr. Green's death. The next day the whole tribe packed up and went to North Carolina. As soon as they left, other ghosts appeared. But these spirits weren't like the others. They were eviler, and they chased people. They dragged the old town drunkard into the forest, and no one ever saw him again. Soon more spirits came. After a while, the whole city was too afraid to go near the property. But your Great Grandfather watched the property from a distance and noticed a pattern. They only came out at night. He wanted to protect the townspeople from the place. After the Cherokee tribe left, he felt a personal responsibility because he'd killed Mr. Green. Soon the stories about the forest got out. Nobody went there. They were all afraid the spirits were hostile. Every person that went into the forest after Mr. Green's death has never returned."

Wilson stood and walked to the window.

"The spirits. Can the spirits see us?"

"Yes, they can see us. But most people can't see them. But you're different. Your eye allows you to see the spirits when you want to."

"Wait. I thought I imagined some of those things. I can see ghosts too?"

"Yes. The only thing you need to remember is that when you use the eye, the evil things become attracted to it."

"Why?"

"I imagine it's the power you have. Spirits dominate in the darkness. Your eye shines a light on who they are and their true intentions. It's a novelty in their world. Most people can't see them before it's too late. You're special."

"I'm special, but what about Michael?"

Michael stood and went to the window.

"Yeah. What about me?"

Grandma Noya pulled both the boys close.

"Listen to me and listen good. If you ever venture outside this house at night into the backyard or the forest, you will die a horrible death. Hell is there. And no matter if you can see them or not, they can always see you. It took your Great Grandfather many years to map out a safe perimeter for this place. He brought in preachers to bless the soil. He bathed the land in holy water every day for five years. His intention was for this place to be a wall between hell and the rest of the world. He did everything he could to protect us. This house has been a haven for many years. It keeps the evil spirits from coming into our world. If you're within these walls, you're safe. They can't penetrate. But if you go outside of these walls, no one can protect you from what comes."

Michael moved closer to his grandmother and wrapped his arms around her waist. Wilson continued to stare out the window into the dark backyard. Flashes of light appeared and disappeared at the edge of the forest.

"This land. It's like a guardhouse, isn't it? To be sure, none of the demons escape."

Grandma Noya smiled.

"I knew you would catch on."

"That's why Nana Ama always stared out of this window. She was keeping guard."

Suddenly, Michael looked up at Grandma Noya.

"That can't be true. Nana Ama is Cherokee, and your father is African American."

Grandma Noya coaxed Michael along.

"So that means..."

"So that means the power came from another place."

Grandma Noya smiled at him again.

"Such intelligent boys. You're right. Nana Ama didn't get the power through her blood. She received it another way."

Wilson remembered how Nana Ama had placed her hand over his eye before she died.

"My Great Grandfather Wilson gave it to Nana Ama before he died. And Nana Ama gave it to me when she touched my face."

"That's right."

"But if you knew that, why didn't you tell mom and dad when I started having problems with my eye?"

"Your dad knows. Your mother doesn't."

"Why didn't you tell her?"

"Did you see the vision? Do you know what she has planned? She won't stay with our family."

"How do you know that? Do you have visions?"

"No, but I can tell by the way she moves...how disconnected she is. She doesn't like our family. She doesn't want a life with us."

Wilson remembered what his mother had told him in the vision.

"Yes. I saw mom in a vision."

"When your mother came here, Nana Ama had the same vision. She told me about it."

Michael was lost. He looked from his brother to his grandmother.

"What about mom? What vision?"

"I'll tell you later, Michael," said Wilson. "What am I supposed to do with this power? Do you expect me to quit school and stay in this house all the time?"

Grandma Noya started laughing.

"No, child. You will continue your life. Your only job is to protect the family for now. The gates of hell are strong. They should hold steady. But...."

"But what?"

The woman turned to Michael.

"Child, could you please go to your sleeping bag next to the bed? I need to show your brother something."

"But why not me too?"

"I have another job for you. Your brother is the only one that can see what I'm about to show him."

Michael frowned and walked over to his sleeping bag and climbed in. Grandma Noya turned to Wilson.

"This will startle you. Prepare yourself."

She moved close to Wilson and wrapped her arm around his shoulders.

"Use your fingers and tap your eyelid twice. Next, look out towards the forest."

Nervously, Wilson raised his fingers to his eye and tapped just as instructed.

Suddenly a red demonic creature with two heads banged against the window. It clawed against the glass with its long knifelike nails. Its glowing yellow eyes widened as it saw Wilson. Suddenly one of its heads let out a scream and bit into the neck of the other creature, severing its head from the body. Black blood sprayed from the beast's neck, causing the monster's whole body to stumble backward. As soon as the body touched the ground, hundreds of black vultures with burning wings of fire lit up the sky. The birds descended on the beast, ripping chunks of flesh from its bones with their razor-sharp beaks and talons.

Wilson clung to his Grandmother, a small whimper escaping his lips. He watched as hundreds of wild dogs covered in blood came from everywhere. They attacked the birds as they feasted on the corpse of the demon. Their deep barks were unlike anything Wilson ever heard in his life. Suddenly all the animals scattered. Wilson looked up in the sky as a giant lizard-like foot came crashing down on the corpse of the demon. Next, hundreds of black lizards started falling from the sky, wriggling on the ground and snapping their hungry jaws, searching for food.

"Please, Grandma. Make it stop," cried Wilson. He couldn't take the sight anymore. It seemed like the hellish world would crash through the window at any minute.

"Tap your eyelid again, and it'll stop."

Just as Wilson was about to touch his eye, he spotted something sprinting towards the house from the forest. He could tell it was a human – a little girl. She was Native American, like him. As the girl drew closer, he could see pieces of the child's face fall off. Suddenly the girl stopped and smiled. She gouged out both her eyes and bit into the fleshy orbs like they were candy using both her hands. She held up one hand and pointed her index finger at Wilson.

"Come play with me," the little girl said as she continued chewing, black slime pouring from her mouth. Wilson couldn't take his eyes off the little girl. He got the feeling that he'd seen her before. Suddenly, Wilson became terrified. He tapped his eyelid, and the strange world disappeared. His Grandmother kissed his cheek and walked over to the bed. Michael jumped up from his sleeping bag.

"What did you see?" he asked Wilson excitedly.

"You don't want to know. It would give you nightmares."

"Cool! You've got to tell me, bro. I won't get scared. I promise you. I won't."

"You didn't see any of it?"

"No. It was like you were just standing there looking out the window. I didn't see anything. Just that same old glow coming from the edge of the forest."

Wilson turned to Grandma Noya.

"I'm sorry. I got scared."

After seeing the terror in Wilson's eyes, Michael squeezed his Grandmother's waist tightly and buried his face into her nightgown. Grandma Noya instantly removed his face from her gown.

"Don't cover your face, child. These creatures are things you and your brother will see. You cannot run from the reality of that place. Fear is the enemy."

Grandma Noya took Wilson's hand in hers.

"Calm yourself, boy. Now is the time for you two to become men."

Wilson took a deep breath and turned away from the window.

"I'm calm now, Grandma."

"There is something both of you need to understand about death. It comes to us all. No one escapes it. Remember. Your good deeds fuel your trip into the next world. If you are a righteous person in this world, you will continue that righteous path into the afterlife.

Conversely, if you do evil, you will continue doing evil in the afterlife. That is the orderly way of our lives, and it continues like this for most of us. That is the way most of the elders have explained it to us. Like a stone rolling down a hill, life continues.

But the *Evil One* is someone for which the elders don't have an explanation. Christians believe in heaven and hell. If you describe his presence in that context, he is the Devil. But our family believes he's just an evil spirit that's doing what he did in life. That is the reason I think the Evil One is Mr. Green. He was a man that took joy in murder and terror. Maybe now he's a spirit that refuses to accept the natural transition into the next level of life. Regardless, it's obvious he wants to continue causing mischief here. Who knows? Maybe he's found a way to manipulate the typical patterns of things to take control of souls. Either way, he's only doing what he has always done."

"I don't understand. Those things that we saw flying around out there. Are they good or evil?"

"Both. Some were good people, and some are bad people. But all those spirits are lost in the world between ours and the other. They've forgotten who they used to be. Now they're being used by the *Evil One*. Their bodies are just shells being used to scare the people in this world. All of that is just theater. Decaying flesh, blood, demonic voices; it's all meant to scare you. The souls tucked inside those monsters were people who didn't find peace. They are restless spirits. They're lost. They are only flying around doing bad things because the *Evil One* is compelling them to behave like that. When my daddy died, this land became sacred.

The demons feared it. Nana Ama was the one who decided to build the house on top of the land. And once she finished building the house, she never left."

"How did Great Grandfather Wilson die? What happened?" asked Wilson.

Grandma Noya looked out into the darkness.

"One night, he was watching the forests when something happened. Maybe he got too close. No one knows. All we know is that Nana Ama found him close to death. She never told anyone what happened, but before he died, he passed his power to her. After he died, she built this house."

Wilson climbed into his sleeping bag.

"It's a lot to take in. You boys get some rest. Tomorrow we'll talk about the good stuff."

"The good stuff?"

"Yeah. Tomorrow, I'll tell you about your powers."

Michael sat up in his sleeping bag.

"Tell us now, Grandma."

"No. Not tonight. We'll talk some more tomorrow. Goodnight, boys."

Wilson closed his eyes and tried to sleep, but he kept seeing the strange world in his mind. After tossing and turning for a few more minutes, he finally fell asleep.

15

Lessons at Breakfast

When the boys woke up the next day, Grandma Noya was in the kitchen making breakfast. Wilson and Michael both stumbled sleepily into the kitchen and sat down at the wooden table.

"Good morning Grandma," they both said.

"Good morning, babies. Did you boys sleep okay? I hope my tales didn't give you difficulties."

Michael stood up.

"Can I open the window, Grandma? It's so hot in here."

"I'm sorry. This old stove is metal, and the heat just stays in here. Go ahead and open the window."

Michael walked over to the window. Just as he did, Grandma Noya turned to Wilson.

"Wilson. Tap your eyelid twice."

"Why?"

"Do it. But after you tap it, hold one of your fingers on your eyelid."

Wilson tapped on his eyelid and held one of his fingers there. The room darkened just as it had before. Grandmother Noya grabbed a knife from the counter and threw it at the child. Everything in the room remained black except the glowing blade as it remained suspended in the air.

Michael turned around and saw the knife spinning mid-air.

"Holy shit!" he yelled. Grandma Noya walked over to the boy and grabbed him by the shoulders.

"Stay where you are, Michael. Don't move."

"But how is he doing that? Why is it so dark?"

"Silence, boy!"

Grandma Noya turned to Wilson.

"Do you feel the knife?"

Wilson understood what she meant. The knife felt like it was in his hand, an extension of his body to be manipulated.

"Yes, Grandma. I feel it."

"Good. Now prepare for the pain."

"What?"

Grandma Noya walked over to the knife block and removed two more knives.

"Prepare yourself."

She threw both the knives at Wilson. Afraid of the blades, Wilson lost his concentration. All three knives struck him in his arm.

Pain shot through Wilson, and he moaned in agony. It felt like someone had ripped his arm off.

"Grandma! Why?" he screamed. Wilson slumped over in pain as the blood dripped from his arm. Michael was beside himself.

"Why are you doing this to my brother? Wilson!"

But Grandma Noya remained calm.

"Do you feel the knife in you? Cutting through your flesh?" she asked.

"Grandma! Why are you doing this?" Wilson asked with tears in his eyes.

"Touch your eye with your free hand and then touch the handles of the knives."

"I don't..."

"Do it!"

Wilson reached up and touched his eyelid again. Next, he felt the handles of the knives sticking out of his arm. There was a loud popping sound, and Wilson screamed.

"Aaaaah! Grandma, I feel…"

Grandma Noya smiled.

"Yes. Accept it. You and the knife are one."

Wilson's hands began to tremble, and he held it up to his face. Soon his hand began to glow red.

"It doesn't hurt anymore," whispered Wilson, a warm feeling coursing through his body.

"Holy shit!" yelled Michael.

Wilson's whole face turned silver, and the one eye began glowing red. Each of his fingers resembled the blades stuck in his arm.

"Grandma…I feel so strong."

"Yes. Now tap on your eyelid. Once."

Wilson tapped on his eyelid with one of the blades in his hand. There was a flash of light, and the room returned to its standard sunlit color. Wilson was his usual self, sitting at the table in his pajamas. Michael stood plastered against the wall trembling in terror. Grandma Noya walked over to the stove and placed a skillet on it. As she poured pancake batter into the pan, she spoke to her grandsons.

"You have many powers that you aren't aware of yet. Unlimited strength, the power to shapeshift, physical regeneration, and the ability to fire energy. Those powers and many more belong to you."

Wilson rubbed his arm, searching for the wounds that had been there. In a few seconds, he spotted the wooden handles of the knives at his feet. He picked them up and looked at them. The blades were gone.

Grandma Noya looked at Michael as he remained frozen against the wall. She walked over and kissed him on the cheek.

"Relax, boy. Your Grandmother would never hurt you. You believe me, don't you?"

But Michael didn't hear his Grandmother. He stared at Wilson, mystified by what he had just witnessed. Finally, Grandma Noya shook him.

"Michael! Snap out of it!"

Finally, the boy came back to his senses. He wrapped his arms around Grandma Noya and began to cry. Slowly, she led him to the table.

"Hush, child. Your brother's fine. Don't worry. I would never hurt either of you."

Wilson wasn't sad. He felt energized.

"Where did the knife blades go?"

"They became a part of you."

"What else can I do, Grandma?"

"I can only tell you what I've witnessed with my own eyes. For months, Nana Ama and I cycled through all she could do. We discovered she could disappear and teleport short distances. She could create creatures from the soil, but they only lasted a few minutes before dissipating. She could bend things with her mind. And this is the most important. She could transform her body into anything she touched."

"You saw her do all these things?"

"Yes. Even though I don't have any of Nana Ama's powers, I helped her discover her strengths and weaknesses."

She walked over to the table and slid two pancakes on each of the boys' plates. Michael was still a little withdrawn and stared at his plate.

"Go ahead and put the maple syrup on the pancakes, boy. Don't be shy."

Michael grabbed the syrup bottle from the center of the table and poured the syrup on his pancakes. Reluctantly, he shoved a large chunk of pancakes into his mouth. Wilson took the bottle from his little brother and started pouring it on his pancakes. Grandma Noya sat down at the table with the children.

"There is something I haven't told you that you need to know."

Both the boys looked at her.

"Something is coming. Nana Ama saw it. I told you earlier that the barrier to hell was strong, but that's not completely true. Something is trying to break it from the inside of hell. I guess it's the Evil One. He's becoming stronger every day. Sometime in your lifetime, he's going to break it."

"What does that mean?"

"Remember what I showed you last night?"

"Yes."

"That world will become this world. Evil will run free in our realm."

"What will happen to us?" asked Michael, finally awake from his daze.

"It means that our family will need to do our best to stop the evil from spreading. Indeed, we must become the gatekeepers between hell and the rest of the planet on a much larger scale."

"But there's only me," replied Wilson. Grandma Noya rubbed his head.

"Yes. But you are powerful and strong like Nana Ama. You will find a way."

Grandma Noya walked back to the stove.

"You boys need to finish your breakfast. Next, I'll teach Michael his part in this."

Michael's eyes widened.

"Me?!"

"Wilson is your brother. Did you think you were free of responsibility? Your job is even more important than his."

Wilson and Michael stared at one another.

"I'm going to shower, boys. Finish your breakfast."

Grandma Noya walked out of the kitchen and down the hall.

"Is she going to stab me too?" asked a terrified Michael.

"I don't think so. You don't have any special powers," replied Wilson. After a second, a wicked thought entered his mind. He stood up from the table and went to place his plate into the sink.

"But you never know. Maybe Grandma Noya will get the ax out back for you."

Wilson left his little brother sitting in the kitchen alone. Seconds later, Michael ran out of the kitchen behind his big brother.

16

Michael's Job

Both Wilson and Michael were in Nana Ama's bedroom looking out into the backyard when their Uncle Charlie walked in.

"Where's mom?" he asked. The boys turned around to look at the man and then returned to watching the backyard in the distance.

"She's hanging some clothes," replied Wilson. He hated his Uncle. The man never bothered saying hello. Like a speeding truck, he crashed into what he wanted. Never mind what other people were doing.

"She told me to come over to teach Michael."

Both the boys turned around.

"Teach me?" asked Michael. "You?"

"Who else, dipshit?"

Wilson piped up.

"Hey. Don't talk to my brother like that."

Charlie snickered.

"It's just a figure of speech lame-o. Come on. You guys need to follow me."

Both Wilson and Michael followed Charlie out the front door. As they walked across the yard and stood waiting to cross the road, Wilson stared at the man in disgust. His colossal belly stuck out like a lister bag full of water. There were patches of puss-filled bumps on the nape of his neck from shaving with a dirty razor. Although they were outside, Wilson could still smell the scent of whiskey floating off the man like gasoline. Wilson shook his head. Although his Uncle Charlie was his father's brother, they were nothing alike. Wilson's father was handsome and professional, a well-spoken man with intelligence. Charlie was the very definition of slouch. His jeans hung halfway off his ass, and he could care less. Why Grandma Noya thought this idiot could teach his little brother anything was beyond Wilson.

The three of them reached the front yard and walked around back to the pigpen. They continued walking into the open field until they arrived at the straw scarecrow.

"Okay. We're here. Michael, you stand in front of the scarecrow."

Michael walked over to the scarecrow and turned around to face Charlie.

"Okay. Now, what?" asked the little boy.

Charlie reached into the back of his jeans and pulled out a knife.

"Now I fucking kill you!" he yelled.

Michael let out a scream and fell to the ground. Wilson was about to touch his eye when Charlie started laughing.

"Take it easy. Take it easy. I was playing," Charlie said as he doubled over in laughter.

Wilson walked over and kicked his Uncle in the seat of his pants.

"Stupid idiot! What the hell is your problem?"

Wilson ran over to his little brother and hugged him.

"It's okay, Michael. Don't worry."

Charlie continued to laugh.

"Aw, that's so cute," he said as he pointed the knife at the children and continued laughing.

"A-le-wi-s-do-di!" yelled a voice from the field. It was Grandma Noya. She walked up to Charlie and slapped the knife from his hand.

"You are supposed to be preparing them. Must you always be so childish? De-de-yo-di!"

Uncle Charlie lowered his head in embarrassment. He picked the knife up and tucked it in the back of his trousers.

"Michael. Come here."

Reluctantly, the child walked over to his uncle.

"Your job is to make Wilson's job easier."

Michael looked confused.

"What do you mean?"

"He is the fighter. The weapon. You will be his guide."

"His guide?"

"Airplanes can fly themselves. They just need someone to sit in the seat to tell the plane where to go. You will do the same thing."

Wilson spoke up.

"How can he do that? He can't see the spirits."

"But he can see you. And if you can see your brother, you can protect your brother."

Charlie walked over to the scarecrow and shoved his hands into its shirt. After struggling for a while, he pulled out a small triangle shaped piece of crystal.

"This will be your weapon."

Charlie dropped the piece of crystal into Michael's palm.

"This is a weapon? I don't have a gun or something?" he asked as he held it up for inspection. Wilson burst into laughter.

"It's not a video game. Come on."

Michael looked through the center of the crystal.

"How do I use it?"

Grandma Noya turned to Wilson.

"Tap your eyelid twice."

Wilson tapped his eyelid, and the field turned dark. Grandma Noya turned to Michael.

"Now put the triangle over your eye and look at your brother."

When Michael looked at Wilson, he took in a deep breath.

"Wow, this is so cool!"

A blue ring of fire encircled Wilson.

"What do you see?" asked Grandma Noya.

"There's a circle of fire all around him," responded Michael.

"As long as you keep the triangle over your eye, you give protection to your brother. Now keeping the triangle on your eye, touch each corner of the triangle with your index finger."

Michael touched the corners of the triangle. Suddenly the triangle became warm and started vibrating violently.

"Don't let go of it. Hold it and center the triangle on Wilson," Grandma Noya instructed. Michael continued to look at Wilson through the triangle. The circle of fire surrounding Wilson burned brighter. Suddenly the ringlet shot three explosive bursts of energy and disappeared. Michael removed the triangle from his eye.

"It's gone. What happened?"

"If spirits had surrounded Wilson, you would've killed them. The energy vaporizes every evil spirit close to Wilson."

"Cool. It is like a video game."

Wilson shook his head at his little brother while Grandma Noya frowned.

"Almost. The only difference being, if you don't use it properly, Wilson could die," Grandma Noya warned. Charlie walked over to Michael.

"It also has a bigger weapon, but we won't activate it today," Charlie explained. Michael's eyes lit up.

"What is it?" he asked while inspecting the back and front of the crystal

"If you tap all three corners of the triangle in reverse, a large ball of energy will rise and then detonate. It'll kill every evil spirit within one mile."

Michael put the triangle in his pocket.

"How did you make this?" he asked.

"I didn't. Your Great Grandfather gave it to Nana Ama after they were married. Your Nana Ama didn't know its power until her husband visited her in a dream. After that, we tested it many times. But we've never had to use it."

"Then how do you know it works?"

"Because your Great Grandfather's spirit told Nana Ama how to use it."

Grandma Noya began walking back to the house.

"The sun is setting. Let's get you some dinner before it gets dark."

Wilson grabbed Michael's hand. Charlie quietly walked behind the group to the house.

17

What She Feels

Grandma Noya sipped her tea and rocked back and forth in her rocking chair.

"I'm going to die one day. You boys need to prepare for that."

The statement was shocking to the boys. Wilson placed his iced tea on the warm evening porch and turned to face his grandmother.

"What do you mean? Now? Later?"

Grandma Noya took another sip of tea.

"It'll come sooner or later, I suppose. No one knows when that day will arrive, but it does. And so, death will come for me."

Michael stood and walked over to his Grandmother.

"Why are you saying this, Grandma? Are you sick?"

She rubbed Michael on the head to comfort him.

"It's just one of those old folks' things. The elders see things clearer than youth. The days become a bit duller. The food doesn't bring about the same jolt of energy it once did. Don't fret. You'll experience it too. But it won't be the end of all things. It's just another part of life."

Wilson studied his Grandma Noya's face before he spoke.

"This has to do with what's behind Nana Ama's house, doesn't it?"

Grandma Noya chuckled a bit before responding.

"You have so much of your Great Grandmother in you, Wilson. You're sharp. Yes. I guess it does have a little to do with what's happening back there."

"What's happening? What do you feel?"

"The barrier separating this world from the realm of evil is constantly being tested. I told you it would break in your lifetime, but the truth is it could break any day now."

"Any day?"

"Yes. That's the reason I've been speeding your education."

"My education?"

"When that barrier breaks, you and Michael will be the only weapon the world has against evil. I have to speed up your lessons. I've never had the sight, but I remember everything I used to help Nana Ama. We must teach you about the limitations of your powers. And Michael, we must teach you how to be invisible to the world. There's so much to do and so little time to do it."

"What will happen when the barrier breaks?"

"You may be here, or you may be in the city with your parents. I don't know. But when the barrier breaks, you'll know it. There may be a loud sound like a million trees breaking, or it may just be a feeling you have. Either way, when it happens, both you and Michael will know it."

"What should we do?"

"If your father is in the house, run to him and lock all the doors and windows. Eventually, you'll see strange things like weird beasts and animals you've never seen before. Your neighbors will be confused. None of the people will think to run before it's too late. And then it'll get worse.

"Worse?"

"The evil will attempt to make the world their domain. Stay put for a few days until the visions tell you how to proceed."

"The visions?"

"Yes. Your eye is good. Remember that. It is always seeking a solution to the problem - a righteous solution. Stay calm and use your intelligence. You'll survive."

"And you, Grandma? Where will you be?" asked Michael.

"When the barrier breaks, I'll be gone. This house will be destroyed and overrun by evil spirits. But don't you fret about me. You'll see me again in the next chapter of your life. Remember. Death isn't the end. It's just another gateway for us to pass through."

Grandma Noya walked down off the porch and peered into the sunset.

"You boys have about ten minutes before the sun goes down. Get yourselves together. You'll be staying in Nana Ama's alone tonight."

Michael objected.

"I don't want to. What if the barrier breaks?"

Grandma Noya stared at the child for a few moments before she spoke.

"Like it or not, evil is coming. It doesn't matter if you're a baby or a man. It won't stop."

Grandma Noya walked past the boys into the house.

"Come on, Michael," said Wilson. "Stop being a baby."

Wilson took his brother by the hand and walked to the road. After making sure that no cars were coming, they crossed the street and climbed the hill to Nana Ama's house.

18

The Opinions of Big Brother

"Can I sleep in your bed?"

Wilson sighed and threw the blanket aside for Michael. Although all the lights were on, Wilson had to admit to himself that he was afraid too. All of Grandma Noya's talk about what lay ahead frightened him (although he'd never let his little brother know that it did).

Michael slid into bed with his brother and wrapped his arm around his waist.

"Where do you think mom is?"

"I don't know. Mom is either at home or traveling."

"We're never going to see her again, are we?"

"Yeah. I think we'll see mom again. But I doubt it'll be any time soon."

"Do you think mom and dad broke up?"

Wilson hesitated. He had to give his little brother truth in small doses. Michael couldn't handle honesty in large quantities.

"I don't think they broke up. But maybe mom and dad are just having a difficult time right now. I guess my eye stressed mom out. Any woman would stress about that, I guess."

Michael thought a moment before speaking again.

"I knew mom and dad were going to break up. I had a dream about it."

"Really?"

"Yeah. I dreamed we went home from school one day and she had left. No words. She just left."

"Good thing for us, your dream isn't real."

"You ever notice how Dad always seemed too normal for her? They're complete opposites. Dad likes nature and isn't bothered by life. But mom? She likes expensive things and having tons of friends."

"That's just her personality."

"I don't know why, but I always got the feeling we were holding her back."

"Yeah. I know what you mean."

"What kind of mom sends their kids down south for the summer and doesn't call to check on them?"

"She just seems too busy for us, Wilson."

The boys thought for a while. Finally, Michael spoke.

"I wish she were here now. I miss her."

"Me too."

"Hey, Wilson."

"What?"

"Do you think I'm a pussy?"

Wilson couldn't help himself and burst into laughter.

"Well? Do you?"

"I don't even know what that means."

"A coward. A punk."

"I think everyone is afraid of something. Even me."

"Yeah, but you never show it. You're like Dad. You always hide what you feel."

"Not all the time."

"I'm the opposite. All I do is act scared. Sometimes even my fear frightens me."

"What?"

"Like when Grandma Noya threw those knives at you? I was terrified."

"Anyone would've been afraid."

"Yeah, but why? Why didn't I get angry? Why did I choose the most baby reaction at that moment? That was pussy as fuck!"

"Look, Michael. You must accept who you are. All the good and the bad. It makes you special."

"Special? What am I, some idiot?"

Wilson turned to face his little brother.

"I never told anyone this, but I'm scared."

"You are?"

"I'm terrified. But you know what?"

"What?"

"If there are a million monsters out there in that backyard, there's only one little brother I want by my side."

Michael cracked a smile and looked away.

"Really? Who is that?"

"You, dipshit."

"Do you think the barrier will break as Grandma Noya says?"

"She doesn't lie. I believe her."

"This is scary."

"All I know is that you and I have to find a way to get through this. If the world is ending, we must be smart and strong. We have to protect each other."

"I won't let anything happen to you, Wilson. I promise."

"And I won't let anything happen to you. Let's try to learn all that we can from Grandma Noya. No more complaining about being scared. Let's be strong for the family."

"Yeah. We can do it."

"Now, let's get some sleep."

"Okay. Goodnight, Wilson."

"Goodnight, little bro."

19

The Fatigue of Fear

Wilson was unable to sleep. The brightness from the overhead light and his little brother's loud snoring was beyond distracting. After removing himself from Michael's tight grip, Wilson climbed out of bed to turn off the bedroom light. As soon as he turned it off, he paused in his tracks. A strange eerie bluish light poured into the bedroom from the window. Slowly, Wilson walked over to the window and peered out. He could see the edge of the forest and the strange lights that flickered in the night. A thick fog was slowly drifting across the lawn towards the house. Wilson turned away from the window briefly and then turned back to face it.

"I'm not afraid of this shit," he whispered to himself. Stubbornly, he sat down in the rocking chair. His fingers twitched as he dared himself to activate his powers. Although he knew hell was just outside their window, there was a part of him that didn't want to hide. The whole thing felt like a game that only he could see, and he wanted to move beyond the nervousness he felt inside his belly.

Slowly, Wilson lifted his index finger to his eyelid and tapped.

There was a flash of light, and then Wilson saw them - dozens of pale dead faces pressed against the bedroom window, all of them staring with big eyes and green ooze leaking from their mouths, pushing and pulling at one another to kill him. Wilson stood and walked closer to the window. His heart was pounding so heavily that he started having difficulty breathing.

"I can't be afraid anymore," he whispered. As he moved closer to the window, the zombielike creatures started jerking and screaming as if electricity was in them. Wilson could see that they wanted to tear him apart. Calmly, he raised his hand to the thick bedroom glass.

"The day is coming," he whispered. Suddenly the group of zombies' heads jerked in unison, and they started looking around. There was a burst of light from behind them, and they all turned to run. After the zombies had gone, one figure remained standing in the center of the field – a little girl.

Wilson recognized her. It was the same child he had seen earlier. Wilson didn't know why, but the girl was scarier than all the other monsters. He quickly tapped his eyelid, and soon the field was empty. As he turned to walk back to bed, the hairs on the back of his neck rose. Wilson could feel the little girl staring at him. He jumped into bed and threw his arm around Michael. After a few minutes, Wilson climbed out of bed for the second time and went to turn on the light. He stayed awake for hours before he finally got the girl's image out of his head. When the sun started rising, he fell asleep.

20

It's Coming

For the next two weeks, Michael and Wilson played war games behind Grandma Noya's house. They started by trying to evade detection in the field behind the pigpen but became sick from the smell and decided to take things into the forest. Grandma Noya provided a watchful eye, making sure that they wouldn't get lost in the woods. But her leash on the boys was almost nonexistent. She wanted them to rely on one another.

"You boys need to move away from the normal relationship of big brother and little brother," she once told them. "You need to become one. You need to know each other's thoughts. Anticipation is how you will learn to protect one another."

At first, Michael was afraid. The forest was dark, and every shadow was an evil spirit out to get him. But after Wilson cast a dissatisfied look at him, Michael pushed past his fear. He wanted Wilson to be proud of him, and so the boys went deeper into the forest. Occasionally, the boys would have to deal with Uncle Charlie jumping out from the shadows to scare them. But after a while, the boys began to work together to evade him. One day they became so good, Charlie was unable to pinpoint their location. Afraid that he'd lost them, Charlie ran back to Grandma Noya to tell her of his blunder. Together, Charlie and Grandma Noya sprinted out of the house towards the forest, expecting the worst. As soon as they got beyond the pigpen, they ran into the boys. Wilson and Michael came walking proudly back from the forest, laughing at the scared look on their uncle's face. Grandma Noya looked at Charlie and burst into laughter.

"Damn fool!" she said while shaking her head and walking back to the house.

"Hey! I did lose them!" exclaimed Charlie as he ran behind Grandma Noya, trying to explain.

"Pussy Boy!" whispered Michael behind his back. The chubby man turned around to face the two boys.

"Watch it! Don't disrespect your uncle!"

After glaring at the two boys for a few moments, Charlie burst into laughter.

"You guys are getting a lot better. I guess I need to watch out for you."

After their moment of "growth," Wilson and Michael spent more time with their uncle. Sometimes the boys would sit with him in Grandma Noya's house and watch television. Charlie pointed out helpful observations to his nephews that they never took the time to notice. One day, the three of them sat watching a reality program, and Charlie pointed out such a thing.

"You ever notice how mostly everyone follows the same pattern when they're telling a lie?"

Both Michael and Wilson looked confused.

Charlie pointed towards the tv.

"Look at this dude. Anyone can see that he's lying. He's giving too much information."

Wilson disagreed.

"That doesn't mean he's lying. Maybe he just wants to give the facts."

"No. Humans are lazy fucks. They never give more than they need to get their point across. Let me show you. What did you eat for breakfast this morning?"

"Oatmeal."

"You see? You didn't say runny oatmeal in a flowered bowl with a stainless-steel spoon, did you?"

"I guess not."

"The same thing applies to this dummy. Cops know when you're lying."

The boys also discovered that their uncle had a wicked sense of humor. While they watched, he took Grandma Noya's snuff box and placed it on the front porch. Their grandmother spent all day rummaging through the house searching for the silver tin box containing her tobacco fix, becoming angrier and angrier. After seeing his grandmother on the brink of destroying the whole house, Wilson walked to the front porch and retrieved the can for her.

"Charlie!" she yelled as she threw a pillow at him. "I know it was you!" Charlie ducked out of the room and ran outside, leaving Grandma Noya fumbling with the embarrassing behavior she'd exhibited in front of her grandchildren.

The lessons the boys learned became more intense as the days went on. Wilson learned more about the tremendous power he had and how to wield it. Grandma Noya taught him how to use his ability to manipulate and destroy. Grandma Noya took him to the forest behind her house and showed him how to lift towering trees out of the ground and rip them to shreds with only a simple movement of his hand. It was an impressive thing to learn, and Wilson was grateful for the lesson, but he was also terrified of it. Possessing that much power made him feel weird and clumsy, like a giant walking amongst fleeing villagers.

One day Wilson attempted to remove a large tree from the ground and failed. He felt like he was losing his childhood to a world no one else could see. Frustrated, he sat down and told his grandmother that he was too tired to continue. Sensing Wilson's struggle with responsibility, Grandma Noya stopped his training for that day. She took him into the house and made him help her prepare dinner. While the two made dinner for the rest of the family, they talked about television shows and which girls he liked in his school. There was no talk of strange beings and superpowers. There was only a grandmother and grandson. Eventually, Wilson addressed his failure in the forest.

"It's not fair. I have so many things I want to do. Why do I have to be the one to sacrifice everything for the benefit of the world?"

Grandma Noya put on her oven mitts and removed the bread from the oven.

"Responsibility chooses who commands it. It isn't the other way around. Other than political office, which I think is bullshit, responsibility almost always chooses the person."

"I don't understand. Can't I just be a boy?"

"You are a boy today, but inside of you is a man. And only you know when the time is right to release that man. What you're learning today is like a child seeing a car for the first time. It's big, and your hands are so small. But one day, you'll accept those special abilities as the right fit. And when that happens, you'll be the man you're supposed to be."

Wilson was confused by what Grandma Noya was telling him.

"Here. Let me make this simple for you. Your powers are eternally attached to your emotions. Always use them in an intellectual capacity. Never use them if you are feeling emotional. If Michael pisses you off one day? You avoid those powers. If your dad grounds you for misbehaving, keep the powers away. One wrong decision could ruin countless lives. But on the other hand, if you see an immediate threat to you and your family that warrants a response using the weapons you possess, then use it. Just remember, use your brain, not your emotions."

Wilson shook his head. He battled insomnia for a few nights before he finally understood what his grandmother was saying to him. When he did, he got the most peaceful sleep he'd ever had in his life.

For Wilson's next lesson, Grandma Noya took the boys to a nearby creek. After taking off her shoes and walking onto the slippery rocks, Grandma Noya filled a plastic bucket with mud and water. She brought it back to the boys and dumped it at Wilson's feet.

"Build something for me."

Wilson didn't understand what Grandma Noya meant and just stared at her with a confused look on his face. Michael was more literal in his understanding and fell to his knees to attempt to build something out of the mess his grandmother had given them.

"Get up, boy! This lesson isn't for you," Grandma Noya laughed. "This is for Wilson."

Wilson fell to his knees. Grandma Noya instantly stopped him.

"Goodness! Am I training a bunch of babies? Use your mind."

Wilson stood and looked at the pile of mud and water.

"Close your eyes. Now tap your eyelid and keep your eyes closed."

Wilson tapped his eyelid.

"Now take your index finger and press down gently against your eyelid."

Wilson followed his Grandmother's instructions and pressed against his eyelid.

"Now, think of the kind of dog you want while continuing to press your eyelid."

Suddenly the mud started to swirl and bubble.

"Whoa!" yelled Michael. "You're doing it, bro!"

Soon Wilson shaped the mud into the form of a dog. Wilson continued to picture the dog in his mind. Soon, he heard two gurgled "yaps," and the miniature dog started running along the edge of the creek. Grandma Noya smiled.

"You're much stronger than your Great Grandmother."

Wilson opened his eyes and watched as the dog made of mud ran along the edge of the water. Suddenly it slipped and fell into the creek and melted away.

"Aw man, why'd you do that?" asked Michael.

"I didn't do anything. It did it by itself," replied Wilson.

Grandma Noya walked to the spot where the dog had melted away and put her toes in the water.

"You can make any creature your mind wants, but it won't last long. You're only supposed to use it as a diversionary tactic. You use it to get away from a dangerous situation or to hide. Nothing more."

"So, the creature isn't real?" asked Michael.

"No. It doesn't even have bones."

"It's still freaking cool, bro."

The next day Uncle Charlie taught the boys how to administer first aid and which plants in the forest were best for healing different ailments. On another day, Grandma Noya performed the Elawatalegi ceremony – a thanksgiving to the spirits for the abundance of crops. She took the boys and their uncle out to a stream at the edge of the forest. Once there, she painted their bodies and built a raging fire. For four consecutive days, they sat around the fire, giving thanks to the spirits for life and their continued survival in preparation for the approaching rough winter. Wilson and Michael hardly understood all the strange words spoken, yet they were respectful and tried to put what they were witnessing to memory. After the fourth day of the ceremony, the boys were so tired they went to Nana Ama's house and went to sleep without thinking about the hell in her backyard. Grandma Noya didn't wake them, and they almost slept for two days.

When Wilson and Michael rose from their slumber, they went to Grandma Noya's house expecting new lessons. Instead, what they found was their overweight uncle sitting in the living room with his jeans unzipped and a six-pack of beer cooling his testicles.

"No lessons today, boys. Your Grandma needs to go to town to sell a couple of the porkers."

"Is she gone?" asked Michael.

"No. Your grandmother is out back, getting them ready."

"Why aren't you helping her?" asked Wilson.

"What? I'm not missing the game today. You guys have taken enough of my time as it is. I need my time."

Michael shook his head.

"You're fucking lazy, dude."

Charlie looked at the two boys, smiled, and let out a disgusting burp.

"Fuck you too," replied Wilson as he stormed out of the house.

The boys found their grandmother standing on the wooden fence surrounding the pigpen poking at the animals with a stick. She saw the boys approaching and smiled.

"Are you boys rested now?"

"Yes," they both replied.

"Good. Mr. Harris will be here with his truck in a few minutes. I'm going to need you boys to..."

Grandma Noya froze and whipped her head around in the direction of Nana Ama's house. Both the boys turned to look across the road.

"What is it, Grandma?" asked Wilson. But the woman didn't respond. Instead, she stayed frozen, looking in the direction of the house. Suddenly she dropped the stick she was holding and took off running.

"Chaaaarlie!" she screamed. Michael looked at Wilson, terrified. The two boys took off running behind their grandmother.

"Chaaaarlie!" their grandmother continued. Charlie stuck his head out the front door and looked at his mother.

"Get your brother on the phone! Tell him to come now! Save the babies!"

Wilson and Michael looked at their uncle and became even more terrified. They had never seen the man look so afraid. Once inside, Grandma Noya grabbed both Michael and Wilson by the arms and took them into her bedroom.

"You two stay here. Don't leave unless you have to go to the bathroom. Otherwise, don't leave this room. Do you hear me?"

"Yes, Grandma," they both responded.

As soon as Grandma Noya left the room, Michael moved closer to his brother.

"Is it happening now?"

"Yeah, I think so. Why else would Grandma behave so crazy?"

"I'm worried about mom. Do you think Dad will contact her before it's too late?"

"I don't know, Michael."

"Is Grandma going to come with us?"

Wilson knew the answer, but he didn't want to tell his brother. Grandma Noya's statement about death said to him that she planned to stay where she was until the end.

The boys stayed in Grandma Noya's bedroom for hours, only leaving to use the bathroom across the hall. When they used the restroom, they lingered in the hallway, hoping to capture some information. They could hear their grandmother speaking to their uncle in the other room, but she spoke in her native language, and Wilson didn't understand what was said. Finally, they gave up and fell asleep in the bedroom.

The next day Grandma Noya came into the bedroom and woke the boys before dawn.

"Get your clothes on. Your father is here."

Michael sprung out of bed.

"Is mom here too?"

"No."

"Why didn't she come?"

"She's working, I suppose. Your father will tell you more when you're on the road."

"You're not coming?"

"No. I have to go to town to sell those pigs today."

Wilson went to his grandmother and hugged her.

"Is this the last time we're going to see you?"

A tear dropped from Grandma Noya's eye, and she kissed Wilson on the cheek.

"Only for a little while. You'll see me again. You can be certain of that. Don't fret, okay?"

Michael ran over and joined the hug.

"You should come with us."

"Don't worry about me. Your Uncle Charlie will look after me just fine. Now, come on. We have to get some scrambled eggs in you before you get on that road."

Grandma Noya left the room, and the two boys cast worried looks at one another. Finally, Michael spoke.

"Grandma Noya's going to die, isn't she?"

Wilson lowered his head and walked out of the bedroom.

"Hey there, boys," said Dustin. "It looks like you boys have gotten nice and tanned on this trip."

"Where's mom," asked Michael, ignoring his father's comment.

"She's home. Where do you think she is? She never comes to pick you boys up. What's wrong with you?"

"The two of you aren't getting a divorce?"

Dustin shot a worried look at Grandma Noya and then turned towards the bags sitting next to the front door.

"Come on and help me load your bags into the car. We only have a little bit of time to eat breakfast if we're going to make it out of here before the roads get cluttered."

Once again, Michael ignored his father.

"I think Grandma Noya is worried. She thinks the barrier is going to break soon."

Wilson interrupted his brother and tried to lessen his little brother's blunder.

"But...we've been safe. I haven't seen anything strange. Have you?"

"No. But you know how the elders are. Grandma Noya can sense stuff."

Grandmother Noya ignored the conversation between the boys and walked into the kitchen. Wilson walked out onto the porch and looked at Nana Ama's house. The old structure looked as spooky as it ever did, but there were no noticeable changes that Wilson could detect. He closed his eyes to see if he could feel something – a change that would let him know of an escalation. But he could sense nothing. Wilson's father walked out of the house and stood behind him.

"You ready to get back to the city?" he asked.

"I could tell you were lying when Michael asked about mom. Where is she?" Wilson asked. Dustin took a deep breath and spoke.

"I don't know where she is."

"Did she leave for good?"

"I don't know. I just came home from work one day, and she was gone. Her clothes are still in the house, so I'm assuming she just needed a few days."

Wilson paused for a few moments and then blurted it out.

"I'm glad she's gone. She didn't want to be here, and I'm not sad that she's not."

Dustin took another deep breath.

"Yeah, you have Grandma Noya's personality in you for sure."

Seconds later, Michael came out of the house.

"What are you guys talking about?" asked Michael.

"Nothing much. You ready?" asked Dustin.

"If I said no, we'd still have to go. So, what's the point?"

Dustin roughed up his son's hair.

"Grab that last bag."

After loading everything in the car, Wilson's father went to Grandma Noya and embraced her.

"Don't be afraid," she said. "I've prepared you for this moment. I just wish I had more time with them."

"Me too, Mom. Take care of yourself. Safe journey."

Charlie walked out onto the porch and embraced Dustin.

"Take care, big bro. Don't worry. I'll look after mom."

Dustin smiled and smacked his brother's belly.

"You're a good brother, Charlie. See you on the other side."

Wilson and Michael looked nervously at one another. Together they ran to Grandma Noya and hugged her.

"We had fun this summer, right?" she asked.

"Yeah, but we're leaving early," said Michael.

"Don't worry. We'll have plenty of summers together."

"Really? You promise?"

"I promise. Get in the car and put your seatbelts on."

Michael ran to the car, but Wilson lingered.

"Explain to him. He won't understand," whispered Grandma Noya.

"I will," replied Wilson.

"You have such a strong spirit. It will be your responsibility to protect the family. Don't worry about your uncle and me. We'll be fine."

Wilson kissed his Grandmother and walked to the car. After he climbed in and fastened his seatbelt, Dustin started the car and pulled away from the house. The boys continued watching their grandmother standing in the yard until she disappeared.

21

A Father and His Sons

"Being here without mom is weird," exclaimed Michael as he poured himself a cup of orange juice. The comment caused Dustin to look up from his newspaper briefly. After realizing that the conversation was one he didn't want to have, he returned to reading the news.

"I mean, we're going to school in a couple of weeks, and we still haven't been shopping for school clothes," continued Michael. Wilson let out a sigh of frustration. Sometimes his brother liked to start fights and now was not the time. Frustrated, Dustin laid his newspaper on the dining room table and spoke.

"Is that what this is about, school clothes?"

"Yeah. I mean, I don't know. It just feels weird without mom here."

"So, what do you want me to do? Chase her down?"

"Shouldn't we? She probably has no idea of what's coming. Shouldn't we at least try to get word to her?"

Wilson stood up and tossed his cereal bowl into the sink.

"Do you always have to be such a prick?"

"Screw you, Wilson! I'm not allowed to be worried about my mom?"

"Why don't you try thinking of someone other than yourself?"

"I am. Why do you think I want to find our mother?"

"Did it ever occur to you that maybe she doesn't want to be found? Women don't just leave their families to go fuck other men!"

Wilson's eyes widened, and his face became warm. He didn't mean to speak so harshly in the presence of his father. But maybe honesty is what his little brother needed to get his mind right. His mother was gone, and she wasn't coming back.

"Look. You boys have to find a way to make peace with your mom's decisions. It wasn't your fault. It wasn't my fault. Some people don't like the family life."

Michael's eyes became watery. With his fists clenched, he yelled at his father.

"Why didn't you try harder? She could've stayed if you didn't argue with her so much!"

Michael put his hands over his face and started sobbing. Wilson moved to comfort his brother, but Dustin shook his head.

"Do not comfort him, Wilson. Michael needs to come to terms with his mother's decision."

Dustin stood up from the table and took his empty glass to the sink.

"When you finish crying, you need to wash these dishes. Starting today, we will take turns at keeping the house clean."

Dustin grabbed his briefcase and walked to the front door.

"I should be home by six or so. Don't let anyone in. Call my cell if you two need something."

As soon as their father closed the door, Wilson exploded.

"Damn, Michael! Why do you have to be such a baby?"

"Shut up!"

"You shut up! Dad is hurting worse than us! Can't you see that?"

"You're only saying that because you're closer to Dad than Mom. He always liked you more."

"How does that help us now? Is that going to bring Mom back?"

"Fuck you, Wilson."

Michael walked to the closet and grabbed his jacket.

"What are you doing?"

"I'm going to the mall."

"But Dad told us to stay inside."

"You can stay where you want, but I'm tired of being stuck indoors."

Wilson moved in front of the door.

"Put your jacket back in the closet."

"You're not the boss of me. I can do what I want."

Wilson waved his fist in Michael's face.

"Don't make me knock you out."

"Do it. I dare you!"

Wilson smacked Michael across the face. As he fell backward, Michael wrapped Wilson's head in a headlock. The two boys tumbled to the floor.

"You don't tell me what to do!" grunted Michael. Wilson struggled to free himself, but Michael's grip was too firm. Frustrated, he punched him in the belly with his fist repeatedly. He heard the air rush out of Michael's mouth, but the boy maintained his firm grip on Wilson's head.

"I'm not a pussy!" Michael yelled as he struggled to fill his lungs with oxygen. Wilson could fill his underarms dripping with sweat as he remained locked in his brother's vicelike grip.

"I never said you were. Let go!"

"You're not the boss of me! Say it!"

Wilson knew he'd never be able to gain big-brother leverage over Michael again if he submitted.

"Fuck you! I'm not saying it."

Michael tightened his grip on his brother's head.

"Say it, and I'll let you go."

"Fuck you. You might as well prepare to keep me locked in forever because I'm not saying it."

At that moment, the phone rang, and both the boys looked at the phone on the table.

"Look! It's probably Dad calling to check on us. Let me go!"

Michael squeezed tighter.

"Not until you say it!"

"I'm not saying shit! But you can best believe if Dad asks why we didn't answer, I'm telling on you."

These words seemed to get through to Michael, and he loosened his grip.

"Go ahead. Answer it, pussy boy."

Wilson kicked Michael in the butt and ran to the phone.

"Hello?"

"Stop fighting."

Wilson smiled, and his eyes lit up.

"Grandma Noya! How are you?"

"You boys don't have time to be fighting one another. You have to find a way to stop viewing each other as brothers and start seeing one another as men."

Wilson looked at Michael, lying on the floor.

"But how did you know we were..."

"Never mind how I know. I'm your Grandmother, remember?"

"Yes, Grandma Noya."

"Now go and apologize to your brother. When you finish, tell him I want to speak with him."

"Okay. Hold on."

Wilson laid the phone receiver on the table and walked over to Michael.

"I'm sorry, Mike. I need to be more respectful of you. I shouldn't have hit you, and I'm sorry about that."

Michael's mouth dropped open.

"It's cool. Don't worry about it. Is that Grandma Noya on the phone?"

"Yeah. Grandma wants to speak to you."

Michael went to the table and grabbed the phone.

"Hello? Grandma Noya?"

Wilson walked into the bathroom and stood in front of the mirror. His eye was feeling strange; it burned, and he was seeing large floaters moving throughout his vision. After moving closer to the mirror,

Wilson pulled open his eyelid with his two fingers. As soon as he did, a small white worm shot out of his eye and fell to the sink. Wilson watched as the white creature wiggled and squirmed around the sink. Finally, he turned on the faucet and watched as the slippery worm disappeared down the drain. Wilson looked into the mirror again, expecting to see another creature in his eye. There was nothing. Suddenly there was a throbbing in his head, unlike any headache he'd ever had. Feeling dizzy and nauseous, Wilson stumbled to his bedroom, fell on the bed, and slept.

22

Charlie's Theory

"Wilson. You awake?" asked Michael as he shook his brother. Wilson sat up in his bed and looked around.

"What time is it?"

"I think it's 8 pm."

"I slept for the whole day? Why didn't you wake me?"

"I tried, but you wouldn't wake up. Dad isn't home yet."

"He didn't come home from work?"

"No. I tried to call Dad, but he didn't answer his cell. I guess he's in a meeting or something."

Wilson grabbed the phone beside his bed and dialed. The call went to his father's voicemail.

"You see? Straight to voicemail."

Wilson's stomach growled.

"You hungry?"

"I'm starving."

"Me too. Normally I'd order pizza, but I don't think we should right now."

"Yeah."

"What about spaghetti? It's easy, and I think dad took out some ground beef to thaw."

"That'll work."

By the time the boys finished their second helpings of spaghetti, Dustin had come walking through the door carrying two large pizzas.

"I see you boys ate dinner. Good. I guess we'll just save this pizza for tomorrow."

"Where were you? We tried calling your cell phone, but it went straight to voicemail," asked Michael.

"I was talking on the phone with your mom," Dustin responded. Wilson looked up at his father and then returned to eating his plate of spaghetti.

"You did?" asked Michael. "What did she say?"

"We talked about a lot of things. She said she's coming home in two days. She's taking a flight out of Paris, and she should be home by Friday. She's had some problems with her credit card. That' why she hasn't called. She just took a few days to figure some things out."

"Really? To stay?"

Dustin looked at his son for a few moments before he spoke.

"We're going to *try* to fix things, but I can't promise that we will. There are a lot of issues that we need to work through."

Michael smiled.

"Well, at least you're trying."

"Yeah. We'll see how things turn out."

Wilson got up from the table and went to wash his plate.

"What about you? No questions?"

Wilson shrugged.

"You can't enjoy the sunshine until the sun comes out. We'll see."

Dustin's eyes widened, and he slapped his son on the back.

"My God! You are starting to sound like your Grandmother."

Dustin grabbed two large slices of pepperoni pizza from the box before heading towards his bedroom.

"I'm going to grab some sleep, boys. Wake me if you need anything. Goodnight."

Michael went to the bathroom and left his brother sitting alone in the kitchen. For a few minutes, Wilson remained seated at the table, thinking about what he'd just heard. He didn't know how he felt about his mother and father reconciling. A part of him missed her, but his mind told him that her return wasn't the sign of a mother missing her family. From what his father had said, her return felt negotiated—like mercy. Flashes of her confession to Wilson still burned brightly in his memory. She'd become pregnant with a child outside the marriage. She'd killed it through abortion as a matter of convenience. Maybe she thought of terminating his life when Wilson was in her stomach. One thing was for sure. He didn't trust her. In the hallucination, she ceased being his mother. And now, he only had a father.

Wilson went to his bedroom and laid on his bed. With so many thoughts swirling around his head, sleep was impossible. Finally, Michael came into the room. As usual, he'd forgotten to dry off. Water was dripping all over the floor.

"She's not coming back, is she?" Michael asked while sliding his wet body into his pajamas. Unable to hide his frustration, Wilson responded coldly.

"No, she's not coming back."

Wilson knew his brother would go to bed crying, but he didn't care. His mother had chosen to abandon them, and Michael needed to accept it. Michael dove on his bed and grabbed a comic book from the nightstand.

"I knew Dad was lying."

Wilson was surprised.

"You did?"

"It's like Uncle Charlie said. He gave too much information. Of course, he was lying. The truth is, Dad probably begged her to come home, and she said she'd think about it."

Wilson smiled.

"My little bro is smart. You're growing up now."

"Ain't no dummies in this family. At least not anymore."

Wilson got up, turned out the light, and jumped back in his bed.

"Hey, Wilson?"

"Yeah?"

"Can I sleep with you?"

Wilson smiled and pulled the covers back. He guessed his little brother wasn't so big after all.

23

The Barrier Breaks

At first, Wilson thought Michael was having one of his bed shaking nightmares. He ignored the shaking of the bed and turned over to go back to sleep.

"Mike. Stop shaking the bed," mumbled Wilson. Suddenly, a thunderous boom violently rattled the bed and caused the closet door to fly open. Wilson sat up and looked around. Although the room was dark, he felt Michael sit up in the bed beside him.

"Wilson! What's that?" his brother asked. Wilson could feel his heart pounding. Suddenly a louder boom sounded, this time sending both children flying into the air. Wilson winced as his face pressed against the ceiling before he fell back down onto the bed. Michael went flying through the darkness and slammed into the closet door. Wilson rolled off the bed and grabbed his jeans from the floor. He stumbled over to the wall and turned on the light. As the bedroom light flashed off and on, the bookcase closest to him shook back and forth violently, dumping books all over the floor. Wilson saw Michael lying on the floor.

"Michael! You okay?" Wilson screamed. After letting out a moan, Michael climbed to his feet and stumbled to where Wilson was standing.

"What's going on? Is this it?" Michael asked.

Just as the house began to tremble again, both boys locked eyes on one another.

"Dad!" they both yelled. The boys stumbled out of the bedroom and into the hall. As they reached the tv room, they saw their dad struggling to maintain his balance at the end of the hall.

"We have to get outside!" Dustin yelled. "The house isn't safe!"

The two boys followed their father through the trembling house. Struggling to maintain his balance, Dustin grabbed Michael by his shirt and tossed him out the front door. After making sure the boy landed softly in the grass, Dustin grabbed Wilson by his shirt and sent him flying into the grass as well. Both boys crawled to the center of their yard and waited for their father to exit. Dustin disappeared into the shaking house and grabbed a bag. After a few seconds, he dove out of the house onto the lawn.

Wilson looked around the neighborhood. Everyone was on their front lawns, watching their houses shaking.

"This is the strongest earthquake I've ever been in," said an elderly man to his next-door neighbor. The middle-aged woman in rollers standing next to him concurred.

"This is the longest earthquake I've ever seen. The aftershocks keep coming. What do you think it is?"

Two teenaged boys flopped down on their lawn to discuss the events.

"It's the end of the world. It has got to be. Just like my vampire comic says."

His friend disagreed.

"Are you stupid or something? This earthquake is a regular one, plain and simple."

Suddenly there was a loud cracking noise in the sky that caused everyone to look up. Wilson watched as a dark violet ball of energy exploded above their heads and released energy across the horizon. The ground stopped shaking, and bolts of lightning began shooting down from the sky.

"Back to the house!" yelled Dustin. Wilson and Michael sprinted to the front door and ran inside. Once they were all in, Wilson peered out the window. The lightning had struck the two boys sitting on the lawn across the street from them, and their corpses continued being struck by lightning repeatedly. Wilson turned to Michael.

"Get the triangle!"

Michael ran into the bedroom and returned carrying the small crystal object his grandmother had given him.

"Wilson!" Michael screamed. "Your face!"

Startled by his brother's words, Wilson placed his palm on his face. After touching his skin, his eyes widened, and he ran to the bathroom mirror. His eyeball was no longer white. It was the same violet color as the sky. There were dozens of thick veins stretching from the corner of his eye down into his cheek. Each vein seemed to pulsate with every heartbeat he had, making his face seem as though it were breathing. Wilson vomited in the sink.

"Dad!"

Dustin and Michael ran into the bathroom and stared at Wilson.

"It's just as she told me. You are the protector," whispered Dustin.

"The protector? Who told you that? Grandma?"

Wilson pushed past his father and ran to his bedroom. He grabbed the phone from the floor and dialed Grandma Noya's number.

Dustin stood in the doorway.

"You can't reach her."

Wilson started to panic.

"Why?"

"She's gone. The explosion took mom and Charlie."

Wilson threw the phone across the room.

"She never told me about this! What is it? What's happening to me?"

"Mom was supposed to tell you."

"She didn't! Now, look at my face! I'm a freak, just like mom said! I'm tired of your secrets! Tell me the truth now, or I'm leaving!"

"There's a book in your Great Grandfather's house. It's a book of ancient drawings that outlines what will happen when the barrier to hell breaks. You're in it."

"I'm in it? What does that mean?"

"The book shows a child with a glowing eye. He saves the world by going into hell."

"You haven't told me anything that makes sense! What's happening to me?"

"Your face is changing because you are gaining more powers. But…"

Dustin looked away from his son.

"But what?"

"As evil draws closer to you, he can sense your presence."

"Who?"

"The Evil One. He knows about you. He's trying to kill you and Michael. Your face and your feelings are the only way he will know who you are. He marks your face with his power, so you are easy to identify to his minions. When they see the mark, they will attack you."

"Why wasn't I told this earlier?"

"Truthfully? We weren't sure if you were the one. Grandma Noya was the only one to sense it. Ever since you were a child, she knew what would happen and tried to prepare you."

"Is there something else I should know? Am I going to grow claws? Am I going to become a hideous monster?"

"No. The only thing that I can tell you is that the eye will guide you. It will tell you what to do through visions and dreams."

Michael walked into the room and sat next to Wilson on the bed.

"You and mom aren't shit," he said as he put his arm around Wilson. "Both of you!"

"The silence I took was to ensure Wilson grew to his complete potential."

"It's still a bunch of horse shit! Everyone has a right to know what their fate is. Who are you to hide that from us? You're no different than mom!"

Dustin walked over to his sons and sat next to them on the bed.

"There are a lot of things in this world that you don't understand. Maybe your mother and I haven't been the best at revealing everything to you, but that's the life of a parent. Finding the proper balance between how much to reveal to your children and what you shouldn't."

Dustin lifted Wilson's chin to look at his face.

"One thing is certain. We should probably get out of here. If your face has changed this much, something is coming."

Dustin went to the window and peered out.

"You boys need to pack your duffle bags. We're leaving in an hour."

"But where are we going? Wilson's supposed to guide us through the visions, right? He hasn't had any."

Suddenly there was a ringing in Wilson's head, and everything began moving in slow motion. He looked at his Dad standing in front of the window and extended his arm to yell out to him.

"Daaaad...Moooove!"

The words came out of Wilson's mouth like a long piece of yarn. Dustin opened his mouth to speak, but nothing came out. Suddenly two hairless dogs with glowing red eyes burst through the window, spraying glass across the room. One animal clamped down on Dustin's wrist while the other sank its fangs into his neck. Both animals pulled him out of the window, and two other dogs burst into the room. They growled at Michael and were about to attack when there was a flash of light.

Wilson was talking to his dad again as he stood in front of the window.

"You boys need to pack your duffle bags," Dustin repeated. "We're leaving in..."

Wilson ran to his Dad and grabbed him by the arm.

"We need to get out of here! Now! I just had a vision!"

Wilson turned to his brother.

"The basement!"

Michael didn't wait. He sprinted down the hall to the basement door and held it open.

"Come on!" he yelled to Wilson and Dustin. They both ran out of the room and slammed the door behind them. Just as they did, they heard the thud of two dogs crashing against the door. Dustin held the door closed.

"Go to the basement. I'm right behind you!"

Wilson ran to the basement door and beckoned for Michael to go down. As soon as his brother was safe, Wilson turned his attention back to his dad.

"Dad! Let go of the door! I have this!"

Dustin looked at Wilson apprehensively. After the dogs quieted behind the door, he let go of the doorknob and took off running towards the basement door. As soon as he did, the hairless dogs came tearing through the door. Wilson tapped his eye twice and extended his hand in a grabbing motion. The dogs rose into the air and remained suspended, barking wildly and snapping their jaws, trying to break free. Wilson slowly closed his fist and squeezed. Blood from the animals shot all over the walls, and the two dead animals fell to the floor. Dustin made it to the door and paused.

"I need to grab some food from the kitchen."

Dustin ran into the kitchen and grabbed a large garbage bag from underneath the sink. He rifled through the cabinets tossing in all the canned food, chips, and bread until the bag was full. Dustin was about to head to the basement but turned back to grabbed a handful of spoons, forks, and a pan from the cabinet. Just as he did, a large shadow walked past the kitchen window. Dustin slowly backed away, keeping his eyes on what was just outside. Suddenly the animal pressed its face against the glass. Dustin's heart got stuck in his throat. The animal looked like a bear, but its face was covered in dozens of eyes, all of them blinking independently and searching the house. Suddenly a woman's scream rang out in the yard. The beast snapped its head around and took off, running towards the sound.

"Quick, Dad! Run!" whispered Wilson. Dustin took one step and paused. He turned around to look at the cabinet closest to the window.

"Wait! I've got to get the gun," he whispered.

Wilson shook his head.

"Forget it! I can protect us! You don't need it!"

Dustin tiptoed over to the cabinet and inched it open. He grabbed the small metal box containing his handgun and the bullets from the top drawer. Slowly, he backed away from the window.

Suddenly the window exploded, and the beast stuck its face through the glass. The creature let out a blood-curdling growl and swung its massive paws at the edge of the window, trying to make room for it to get inside. Dustin ran across the room to the basement door and went inside. He quickly retrieved his car keys and locked the basement door while Wilson and Michael stared at him from the bottom of the stairs, terrified. There was a thud against the door as a shadow moved underneath it. The monster lowered its nose to the crack and began to sniff. Dustin ran down the stairs and grabbed a can of paint from the bookshelf. He took a lighter from his pocket and began spraying the paint. As soon as Dustin placed the flame in front of the spray, flames started shooting from the can. He quickly ran up the stairs, aimed the fire underneath the door, and continued spraying. The children watched as the bottom of the door caught fire.

"Dad!" yelled Michael. "The door!"

Still, Dustin continued spraying. The monster let out a scream and smashed its paws against the door. Dustin stopped spraying and backed away from the door. After a few seconds, the beast let out a painful moan. Slowly, the creature moved away. Dustin ushered the boys over to the sofa sitting in front of the television.

"We'll hold up down here."

Wilson lowered his face into his palms. The pain coursing through the side of his face was excruciating. It felt like a thousand fire ants were crawling beneath his skin. Suddenly the room began to dim. Unable to sit up anymore, Wilson fell back on the sofa and fainted.

"Wilson?" asked Michael. When his brother didn't respond, Michael began to panic.

"Dad! Wilson!"

Dustin went over to Wilson and looked at his face.

"We can't stay here long. The demon is close."

"But where are we supposed to go? Wilson is supposed to guide us." Dustin looked around the room.

"Go to the bathroom and get a towel. Wet it and bring it back so we can keep your brother cool."

As soon as Michael ran to the bathroom, Dustin kneeled over his son and whispered.

"Let the ancestors guide you."

24

Finding His Way Through Dreams

Wilson knew he was dreaming. Although his dream had the same surreal feel as all the others, his senses knew it was a dream. It was midday, and he was sitting in the front seat of his father's car at an old gas station in the middle of nowhere. The car's inside was stifling, resulting from his father turning off the car engine to pump gas. A strong wind was blowing up dust clouds, making it difficult to see his father pumping gas into the car. Wilson sat in the front seat with a cold soda on his lap. Potato chip crumbs covered the front of his jeans, yet he continued digging into the large bag to shove handfuls of chips into his mouth.

"I said you could have *some*, not all of them," complained a familiar voice from the backseat. Wilson turned around to see his brother with an extended arm beckoning for the bag of chips. His father was wearing an old cowboy hat, which seemed to be three sizes too big for him. His father pushed up the gallon-sized hat to see the prices on the pump as the car appeared to drink an endless amount of gasoline.

Suddenly, a red convertible sports car pulled into the gas station. Wilson could tell by her long brunette hair sticking out from underneath her sunhat that the driver was a woman, but he couldn't see her face. As if she were a race car driver, the woman stood up in the driver's seat and leaped out of the car, her floral dress blowing in the dusty wind.

She ran up to the vehicle Wilson was in and yanked the gasoline pump out of the tank. Wilson tried to look at her face, but her sunhat shadowed her face. Suddenly, she slapped her open palm against Wilson's window to get his attention. Slowly, he lowered the window.

"You can reach me if you hurry! My plane is in t*hat* city," her soft voice said.

"What city?" Wilson asked.

The woman pulled off the hat and smiled – it was Wilson's mother!

"The mountains are safe. That thing hasn't come here yet, but it's moving fast. You can reach me before it does."

"Where are you?"

Suddenly his mother reached into her bosom and pulled out a gun.

"Get out of here!" she yelled. Wilson turned around to see where she was aiming her gun. A large black cloud appeared on the road from far away. Wilson yelled for his father, but nothing came out of his mouth.

"Forget about him!"

"No! That's my Dad!"

"They're going to kill him anyway. He's of no use to you!"

Wilson watched as his mother started firing bullets into the dark cloud.

"He's coming for you! There isn't much time! You have to leave now!"

Wilson started searching for his father, but he couldn't find him.

"Dad! Where are you?" he screamed. Suddenly the car started, and the engine revved. Wilson looked in the driver's seat. Michael had started the car.

"Time to get the fuck out of Dodge," the little boy said. He stood up on the gas pedal, and the car shot out of the gas station towards the road.

"What are you doing? We can't leave Dad!"

Michael reached into his jacket and pulled out a pack of cigarettes.

"Shit's fucked up, Wilson. But don't you worry. I'll take care of those fuckers. Here, grab the wheel."

Wilson grabbed the steering wheel and steered the car along the empty road. Michael stood up and grabbed the triangle from his pocket. Like a madman, he started firing lasers into the black cloud. Suddenly lightning started shooting out from the cloud in all directions.

"I got those fuckers for you, bro."

"Where's mom?"

"What?"

"She was standing by the car!"

Michael sat back down in the car seat and took a long drag on his cigarette.

"Shit's fucked up, bro."

Suddenly, Michael slammed on the brakes, and the car screeched to a halt. A herd of buffalo stood in the middle of the road.

"Go around them!" screamed Wilson. Michael stood up in the car seat again and yelled towards the herd of buffalo.

"Huh? What?"

Wilson was terrified. The cloud was getting closer.

"What are you doing? Let's get out of here!"

"She's where? North Carolina? Where? Asheville?"

Suddenly, the animals turned towards the vehicle and started charging.

"Back up! Back up!" yelled Wilson. Michael turned and smiled at his brother.

"Why are you afraid? Death is only the beginning."

Suddenly, the herd of buffalo crashed into the car.

25

The Getaway

Wilson sat up on the couch and removed the towel from his head. Michael was sitting at the end of the sofa while his dad was standing in front of the tv.

"How long was I out?" he asked Michael.

"Not long. Ten minutes."

Wilson stood up and walked to his dad.

"I know where we're supposed to go."

"Where?"

"North Carolina."

Michael walked over to them.

"North Carolina? Who do we know in North Carolina?"

"Mom's there."

"She is? But I thought she was in Paris."

"Her plane got sidetracked. That's where she is."

"But how are we going to get to her? Look at the news."

Wilson watched as people got attacked by strange creatures that he'd never seen before. A news reporter attempted to give a report and was bitten in half by what looked like an enormous lizard. Another video showed a child being chased by wild dogs before the large animals caught him and ate him alive. A man attempted to fight off a slimy black creature with long teeth and glowing red eyes. The man fired his gun and hit the monster twice in its chest. Unfazed by the weapon, the beast released a burst of red lasers from its eyes and vaporized the man. Another video showed two corpses jumping on an elderly woman and biting into her face until she stopped moving.

Suddenly, Wilson felt a sharp pain in his face, and he bent over. He went to the bathroom and looked at himself in the mirror. His face was getting worse. The veins covered all his face, and his other eye was bloodshot. He walked back out to his father and brother.

"We need to leave. Now! Grab the food. Mike, I need you to get your weapon ready. I'm going upstairs to get the car."

Michael looked scared, but Wilson knew his brother was ready. He'd seen that same determined look on his face when they played video games. Accepting that his sons were the leaders, Dustin grabbed the bags and headed to the stairs. He stepped aside on the stairs to let both Wilson and Michael pass. Wilson turned to his brother.

"Remember what Grandma Noya told us. Your job is to protect what I can't see. Okay?"

"Don't worry about me, bro. Let's do it."

Wilson opened the door and immediately saw the mouth of a giant snake as it stood up to bite him. As if it were nothing, Wilson extended his open hand like he was grabbing something. As he closed his fist, the snake's head crumpled in on itself, and the snake fell to the floor. Wilson took one step and saw an animal that looked like half-human and half-bird. Its body was human, but its skin had feathers. It had a large beak that opened and closed, revealing a tongue with eyes. Wilson tapped his eyelid, and his eyeball began to glow. He held his breath and flexed his ribcage. After aiming at the creature, Wilson pushed outward through his eye. A long stream of fire shot from his eye and engulfed the monster in flame. Wilson turned to his little brother.

"Put your back against mine! If anything attempts to attack me, you kill it. If something tries to attack you, say my name, and I'll jump in to attack."

"That's a bet!"

The two boys put their backs to one another and inched through the kitchen and into the living room. Several of the large wild dogs tore through the hallway towards the boys. Michael was ready. He placed the beasts in the center of the triangle and pressed a corner. The wild dogs started shaking and glowing violently until their bodies exploded, sending blood and intestines everywhere.

"This fucking shit is cool!" yelled Michael. Wilson paused and beckoned to his father that it was safe to come out. Dustin took off running and met the boys at the front door.

"Dad, give me your keys."

Dustin handed his car keys to Wilson and threw the bag of food over his shoulders. Wilson readied himself and grabbed the doorknob.

"Okay. One...two...three!"

Wilson swung open the door and took off running towards the car parked in the driveway. Just as he did, the ground opened behind him, and thousands of glowing spiders crawled out of the earth.

"Wilson! Watch out!" screamed Michael. He put as many creatures as possible into the center of his triangle and pressed on each corner. Ooze and spider blood splashed everywhere. Suddenly Michael froze. There were monsters all over the neighborhood, and they all turned towards them.

"Wilson! Hurry!"

Suddenly there was a scream, and all the monsters turned to look up into the sky. Wilson yelled to his brother.

"It's him! Let's go!"

Michael remembered what his grandmother told him about the weapon. Quickly he tapped all three corners of the crystal triangle. Suddenly it started glowing and shaking in his hand.

"Let's go, Dad! Once this goes off, we only have a certain amount of time to get away!"

Dustin and Michael ran to the car and jumped into the passenger side. After grabbing the keys from Wilson, Dustin started the car and peeled out the driveway. As the car turned onto the street and accelerated, a dog with the head of a human baby gave chase.

"Holy shit!" Michael yelled. The sight of the hybrid monster made Wilson want to vomit. He raised his hand and crushed the animal into a heap of mush and bones in the road without looking. The triangle that Michael was holding began to buzz and vibrate more violently. There was a spark of light, and suddenly the weapon released a red ball of energy that rose to the roof of the car and began to burn a hole in it. Michael ducked down in the backseat.

"Were you supposed to activate that thing in the car?" yelled Wilson. As sparks rained down from the roof of the car, Dustin crashed into a mailbox. Everyone exited the car as smoke poured out. They all watched as the red ball of energy grew massive as it rose high into the sky. Suddenly, all the monsters turned to run.

"Look at them running!" yelled Michael. "Run, you bitches!"

"You almost took us out, too!" yelled Wilson. Michael shrugged.

"Grandma Noya never told me how this thing would work," he confessed.

"Get back in the car," said Dustin. Both boys climbed back into the car. Dustin floored the gas, and the car raced out of the neighborhood and made a turn onto the highway. Just as it did, a loud explosion rattled the vehicle, and everything plunged into darkness. Cautiously, Dustin slowed down and pulled the car to the side of the road. Seconds later, the light returned.

"Wow!" exclaimed Michael. Wilson looked around the highway. There were hundreds of dead monsters lying everywhere. Dustin opened the car door and climbed out to look at the carnage.

"I didn't know there were so many of them."

Wilson didn't budge. Instead, he yelled at his father.

"Dad, we need to go if we're going to get to mom before the same thing happens there."

Dustin climbed back into the car and pulled out onto the highway. He frowned as he drove over the corpses of the dead animals littering his path. Eventually, the road cleared, and he was able to increase his speed. Michael exhaled and let his head fall back onto the backseat. He looked up at the giant hole in their roof and smiled.

"North Carolina? Good! Anything to get out of here!"

Wilson laid his head against the window. The pain in his face had mostly disappeared. He closed his eyes and prepared for the long trip. He hadn't realized that he missed his mom so much.

26

Judgment

"Where are we supposed to be going?"

"Asheville."

Dustin looked at the GPS on his cell phone and frowned.

"Asheville? That sounds like a very country place. Do they have an airport?"

"I'm only telling you what the dream told me. It wasn't detailed."

Dustin mumbled and continued driving. Wilson lowered the visor and looked at his face in the mirror. Although his right eye was still bloodshot, his other eye had returned to normal, and the veins in his face were gone. Wilson tilted the mirror and looked at his brother in the backseat. Although the wind was blowing into his face from the hole in the roof, Michael snored like a baby. Wilson grabbed his father's cell phone and searched the internet.

"I'm surprised we still have cell phone service. The only thing on the radio is that emergency warning recording."

Wilson found the airport address and typed it into the GPS.

"I found the airport."

"Good. I was hoping we didn't have to stop to get directions from anyone. We should enter and leave as quietly as possible."

"Leave? I'm not sure we're supposed to. I didn't see anything about leaving in the dream."

"We'll let you rest. I'm sure you'll get another vision sooner or later."

Dustin continued driving until he was within a few miles of the airport. As he got closer, he yelled at Michael.

"Hey! Wake up! We're almost there."

Michael woke up and wiped the drool from the corner of his mouth. After spotting the bag of food on the seat next to him, he reached in and ripped open the box of donuts.

"Anybody want a donut?" he asked. Wilson held up his hand, and Michael passed him one. Dustin ignored his sons. They had arrived at the airport.

"We need to get in there quickly. We don't know how much time we have," said Dustin as he climbed out of the car. Wilson shoved the donut into his mouth and wiped his sticky finger on his jeans. His brother hopped out of the car and followed his father. As they walked close to the entrance, Wilson could see a large group of angry people yelling and screaming at a row of police officers blocking access to the building. Dustin and his sons weaved through the crowd until they made it to the entrance. A woman was arguing with one of the police officers.

"I'm sorry, ma'am, but you can't come in."

"My flight leaves in thirty minutes. Let me in!"

"You can call the airport for a refund. All flights are grounded."

"Grounded?! What do you mean?"

"Haven't you been watching the news?"

A short chubby man interrupted the police officer.

"My daughter's flight landed an hour ago. She's only twelve years old. I need to pick her up."

The officer shook his head.

"You can't go in. We're going to release everyone from the building within the hour."

The man exploded.

"You all have been telling me that for over an hour!"

Suddenly, another police officer moved close to the man and extended his baton.

"Sir, you need to back up before we arrest you."

Dustin grabbed Wilson and Michael by the collar and pulled them away from the building. He walked to the car and dialed his wife's number.

"Hello? Julia?"

Dustin put his cellphone on speaker.

"Julia?"

"Dustin?"

"Where are you?"

"I was on my way home when our flight got diverted to another airport. Something about a national security issue."

"Where's the airport?"

"Somewhere in Asheville."

"We're here. Outside in the parking lot. Come out."

"Wait, how did you know..."

"It's a long story. The boys are with me."

"Hi, mom!" yelled Michael.

"Hello, mom!" yelled Wilson.

They could hear their mother crying.

"Hi, boys. I'm coming out soon, okay? Dustin, take me off speakerphone."

Dustin took her off the speaker.

"Yeah."

"I'm scared, Dustin. They're all kinds of stories going around about invasions and attacks."

"Did they say when they were going to let you all out?"

"It should be any minute."

Suddenly the phone went dead.

"Hello? Hello? Julia?"

Dustin tossed the cellphone onto the seat.

"It's dead. Shit!"

Wilson and Michael stared at the entrance of the airport, expecting their mother to emerge.

"She said she would be out any minute. They're just waiting."

"Waiting on what?"

"I think it's some kind of security procedure they have to go through."

There was a movement amongst the crowd standing in front of the building that caught Wilson's eye. An elderly woman fell to the ground and started convulsing. Then another person fell. And another.

"Look, Dad! Something's happening!" yelled Wilson as he opened the passenger door and stood to get a better look. Dustin climbed out of the car and looked. Suddenly the double doors opened, and people started running from the building.

"There's Julia! I see her!" yelled Dustin. Julia was screaming as she exited the building. Frantically she looked around the parking lot while dozens of people pushed her, almost causing her to fall. Dustin jumped in the car and started pressing the horn to get her attention.

Wilson looked inside the airport through the glass doors.

"They're here!" he yelled.

Hundreds of large hairy spiders with large fangs came crashing through the glass and started crawling all over the building. The creatures let out a hissing sound as they moved through the crowd grabbing their victims and tossing them back towards the larger group of spiders exiting the building.

"Jesus Christ!" yelled one of the police officers. He took out his weapon and started firing at the enormous spider moving towards him. The spider lifted its two front legs and pushed the officer to the ground. Two other spiders jumped on the man and plunged their long knifelike fangs into his body, and sucked it dry of blood.

Wilson saw a small boy being stepped on by the fleeing mob of people. Two large spiders saw the child struggling to climb to his feet. The creatures started crawling towards the child and snapping their venomous fangs. Quickly, Wilson tapped his eyelid. He didn't see the spiders anymore. Instead, in place of the spiders, he saw ghostly spirits with twisted faces. The ghosts plunged their hands into the chests of their victims and ripped out their souls. Afterward, the ghouls put the victims' souls into glowing sacks that each of them carried on their waist.

Wilson tapped his eye again, and the daylight returned.

"They're not spiders. They're demons stealing the souls of everyone they kill. We've got to get to mom!"

Suddenly, a large spider with red eyes knocked a small boy to the ground and jumped on his back. Wilson tapped his eyelid again and extended his hand. The child underneath the hairy spider closed his eyes and prepared to be killed by the demon. Wilson grabbed the monster, twisted its neck, and hurled it over the building. Two other demons approached the child, but Wilson grabbed them and smashed them into one big mush before throwing them over the building as well. Wilson turned to Michael.

"Come on! Let's get mom!"

"Bro! Your face!"

Wilson lifted his palm to his face and felt. The veins had returned. Still, there was no time to worry if he wanted to save his mom. He saw two of the demons moving towards her.

"Shoot the two demons closest to mom!" Wilson yelled.

"Demons? I only see spiders!"

"I see them as demons, but you see them as spiders. Don't worry about that. Shoot anything that looks like it's getting close to mom!"

Michael placed the triangle over his eye and centered it on the spider. He pressed one of the corners, and a laser shot from the triangle and exploded the creature. The remaining spider jumped on Julia's back, and she fell face-first onto the ground. Once again, Michael centered the triangle on his target and fired the weapon. The creature exploded, covering his mother in the thick green liquid. Just as Julia got up to run, another spider was in front of her. Michael quickly fired again.

"I'm going to use the big weapon," he said to Wilson. His brother put his hand over the triangle and lowered it.

"Don't! Something tells me that we're going to need it in a few minutes."

Dustin ran for his wife. As soon as he reached her, another spider attacked. Michael quickly shot the creature and yelled at his father.

"Hurry up, Dad! I can't hold them back!"

Dustin grabbed Julia by her hand and pulled her to her feet. A spider jumped in front of the couple, but Dustin was ready. He pulled out his gun and fired three shots into the spider's head. After killing the creature, Dustin pulled his ooze-covered wife to the car, and they climbed in.

"What the hell is going on?" Julia screamed. Michael hugged his mother and started crying.

"I can't believe we saved you!" he cried as she kissed his face.

"Hi, mom!" said Wilson. Julia let go of Michael and stared at Wilson's face.

"Jesus! Your face! Your eye!"

"It's not permanent, mom. I'll explain later."

"Dustin! You son of a bitch! Did this happen when he went down south?"

Wilson interrupted his mom.

"It's not Dad's fault. Please, Mom. Stop."

Dustin sped out of the parking lot and made a turn onto the road to exit the airport. Wilson looked in the rearview mirror.

"Oh my God!" yelled Wilson. Dustin looked in the rearview mirror while everyone else turned around. Standing in front of the airport was a tall shadow-like figure. It had no face and had long stringy brown hair with two glowing orbs where its eyes were supposed to be. Although the creature had a muscular build, it seemed to be a giant, towering over the airport building, making the fleeing people seem like children running away.

"What the hell is that?" asked Michael. Wilson knew who it was. It was the *Evil One* Grandma Noya had mentioned. Julia began crying and hyperventilating.

"Why is this happening? What's going on?"

Dustin looked in the rearview mirror as the car accelerated. The car clipped the side mirror of an oncoming car and bounced onto the sidewalk. Dustin steadied the steering wheel and turned the car back onto the road.

Wilson looked back at the giant shadow. Although the creature had stopped moving, it seemed to be staring at their car as they tried to make their getaway. The creature extended its arms to the sky and let out a high-pitched scream. Suddenly a wide hole formed in the center of its chest. Wilson watched in horror as thousands of creatures from hell burst from the shadow's body. Large black wolflike creatures with sharp fangs and long claws grabbed the nearest person in sight and shredded their bodies to pieces; demonic creatures with wings made of fire flew high into the sky and began raining fire down on everything causing the nearby forest to start burning.

"Dad. Go!" yelled Wilson.

The ground began to tremble as the monsters ran after the car. Dustin turned his attention to the road and tried not to look back. Although he had the pedal pressed to the floor, he tried to go faster. He dodged oncoming traffic and raced ahead of several vehicles in front of him. Suddenly, Wilson crawled into the backseat.

"Go up front with Dad!" Wilson said to his mother. After pausing a moment to look at the monsters in the sky, Julia climbed into the front seat. As soon as his mother was gone, Wilson tapped his eye. What he saw made him tremble in fear. Total carnage was on the road behind their car. Not only were there monsters in the sky and running after their car, but some creatures were also invisible to everyone else. They were thin human-like creatures with translucent, see-through skin. Wilson could see their black hearts pumping black sludge through the various colored veins within their bodies. Some of the beasts had two heads, and some had one. They didn't run but instead seemed to glide through the air in pursuit of their victims. Each time the creature fell upon a person, it would yank open the person's mouth. It thrust its long tongue in, and the tongue would disconnect from the beast, suck the person dry from the inside, and burst from the person's stomach as a smaller version of the see-through creature. A few seconds later, the demon would grow to adult size and try to repeat the attack.

As the creatures drew closer to the bumper of the car, Wilson extended his hand. He grabbed several of the galloping wolf creatures and smashed his hands together. The two demons yelped and were instantly a pile of mush on the side of the road. Wilson repeated this with ten other creatures. When he turned around to yell to his father, he saw his mother staring at him, unable to speak. Wilson ignored his mother's catatonic state and turned to Michael.

"Hey! You..."

But Michael already had his triangle out.

"I'm way ahead of you, bro. Just tell me when you want me to let go of the big one."

Michael aimed his triangle and started destroying the closest creatures. Wilson smiled. He was proud that his little brother had become an expert at using the weapon. Wilson extended his hand to the thin monsters floating in the distance. As soon as he tried to close his hand, he felt a sharp pain shoot up his arm.

"Ahhhhh..." he screamed as he pulled his hand back. His hand burned.

"Wilson! You okay?" asked his father from the front seat.

Michael was scared.

"Bro! Are you okay?"

"Don't worry about me. I'm fine. Keep shooting."

Wilson lifted his hand and looked at it. There were blisters on it. He shook his hand and put his arm underneath his armpit. In a few seconds, the feeling in his hand returned.

"Okay, Michael. Use the weapon."

"You sure?"

"Do it. We have to get out of here."

"Dad! Pullover!"

Dustin pulled over the car. Michael climbed out, aimed the triangle into the center of the monsters in the distance, and touched all the triangle edges. A flash of light shot from the triangle and a red orb rose into the air. As it got higher, the ball of energy grew larger and larger. Michael jumped back into the car.

"Floor it, Dad."

Dustin sped back onto the road. As the car got further down the road, Wilson looked back at the creatures – they all had turned and started running back towards the shadowy figure. The Evil One let out a scream and turned away from the orb. He raised his hand and slowly faded away against the building. Finally, the sphere exploded, and all the creatures fell like corpses to the ground. Dustin didn't stop. He continued driving until he was back on the highway.

"Does someone want to tell me what the hell is going on?" asked Julia. Dustin exhaled.

"It's a long story. The first thing we need to do is find a gas station. We're almost out."

Dustin drove for an hour before he stopped at a gas station without many people. Everyone got out of the car and went into the convenience store while Dustin pumped gas into the vehicle. After relieving themselves in the bathroom and picking up a few snacks from the store, the boys returned to the car and waited for their mom to come back. Finally, she returned, looking pale and confused. When she climbed into the car, she avoided eye contact. Instead, she put on her seatbelt and looked straight ahead. After a few moments of silence, Michael spoke.

"Where do we go now?"

The question startled Wilson, and he searched his father's face for an answer. Finally, Dustin responded.

"I think we should probably drive on until nightfall. Then we should probably pull over and sleep."

As Dustin pulled out onto the road, he looked over at Julia.

"You okay?"

"I'm just trying to understand what's going on."

"I'll fill you in after we get some rest."

"I'll fill you in after we get some rest."

27

The Way You Sleep

"Dude, do you want a bologna sandwich?"

"No. You spit in it. I know you did."

Michael shoved his index finger deep into his nose and pulled out a long green booger. He opened the sandwich and rubbed it on the pink meat before passing the sandwich to Wilson for a second time.

"Go ahead, bro. We're brothers."

"That's gross! I'm not eating that."

Michael shrugged and took a bite of the sandwich. After chewing it for a while, he smiled and swallowed.

"Sweet."

Suddenly Julia turned to face the boys from the front seat.

"I know a place just up the road where you can do it."

"Do what?"

"Kill yourself."

Wilson was confused.

"What?"

Dustin lowered the rearview mirror and looked at Wilson from the front seat.

"You want to die with your mother, don't you?"

"No."

Michael fumbled under the driver's seat.

"Wait. I can help."

Finally, he pulled out a toy doll. The toy had blond hair, and both the plastic eyes were missing.

"Here. Put this in your mouth."

Wilson looked at his brother and then looked at what was in his hands. The doll had become a handgun. Julia smiled and clapped her hands.

"Go ahead. Put it in your mouth," Wilson's mother squealed. Dustin and Michael joined in.

"Yeah! Go ahead and do it!"

"Please, bro, you've got to do it!"

Wilson lifted the gun to his lips. Just as he opened his mouth, a veiled figure swung open the car door.

"Get out!" the masked woman whispered. Wilson was afraid.

"Where are we going?"

"You'll see."

Wilson climbed out of the car and began walking behind the lady. Although he couldn't see her, he could hear the sound her long black dress made as she took each step – a swooshing sound like polyester fabric between a fat man's legs. Suddenly the woman began speaking to Wilson as they walked. Her voice was as light as a feather, a whisper amongst the trees.

"He approaches from the North. The best way to stop him is by attacking him through the South."

"Who?"

"You will need her. Do not underestimate the Evil One's capabilities."

"Who will I need?"

The woman stopped at the edge of a lake. Although it was dark, a yellow moon was immense in the night sky. Wilson turned to face the woman.

"Who are you?"

He reached for the woman's veil and brushed it aside, but all he could see was more fabric. The woman pointed towards the water.

"The Jellybeans are hidden in the field."

Wilson's eyes widened as he looked into the water. There were large glowing lights at the bottom of the lake.

"What are those?" he asked as he pointed at the large white lights moving on the floor of the lake.

"You will need them."

"Why?"

"What color is pain?"

Suddenly, the woman reached out and grabbed Wilson by his neck.

"Hey! What are you doing?" he gagged. Wilson swung at the lady, and his hand disappeared into the cold fabric like the woman was invisible. As Wilson struggled to free himself, the woman lifted him from the ground and threw him toward the center of the lake. Wilson fell towards the water. Wilson seemed to move in slow motion. He twisted his body to look back at the woman, but she was gone. He looked down into the water and was amazed. The lights at the bottom of the lake weren't lights at all. They were glowing buffalo. Wilson closed his eyes and prepared for impact, but it never came. There was only the sound of a breeze blowing through the trees. Wilson opened his eyes and discovered he was standing on Grandma Noya's front porch. He looked across the street at Nana Ama's house, sitting on the hill. Red lights flashed off and on within the home while vast plumes of smoke billowed up from behind it. There was a tap on his shoulder, and Wilson turned to see Grandma Noya.

"Don't worry about me. My journey was a peaceful one."

"It was?"

Wilson could feel sadness inside of him, trying to get out. He wanted to embrace his grandmother, but he knew he was dreaming. Grandma Noya nodded towards the house on the hill.

"You know you're going to have to go in there, don't you?"

"I don't want to."

"It's the only way they'll return."

"Who?"

"The buffalo. It has always been about them."

Wilson kissed Grandma Noya on the cheek.

"I miss you, Grandma."

She smiled and touched Wilson's face. Wilson turned to look at the house, and this time he was standing in front of Nana Ama's house. The flashing red lights were gone. Wilson looked into the windows of the house and became terrified. There were dozens of white rotting faces pressed against the glass.

"Who are they?" he asked. But his grandmother was gone. Instead, an elderly black man with a long gray beard stood next to him.

"You need a key," he said. As he rubbed his beard, Wilson noticed the chains on his wrists.

"Are you my Great Grandfather?"

"You need a key."

"Where do I find it?"

The man turned and pointed back towards Grandma Noya's house.

"Back there. Through the forest. I buried it in the only place I could hide it."

"In my Great Grandfather's house?"

The old man smiled.

"He can't touch you there. The ground is blessed. It is hallowed soil."

Wilson turned and started walking back towards Grandma Noya's house. After taking one step, he fell into a deep hole. As Wilson fell, he heard voices whispering in his head.

"Wake up...wake up....wake up..."

28

Truth and the Wall

Wilson woke up to a fight. Dustin parked on the side of the road, and his parents were in the front seat, yelling and screaming. Michael sat silently beside Wilson in the backseat, staring out into the darkness with a look on his face so sad that Wilson thought he was going to cry. The look on his face told Wilson how much the argument had damaged him.

"Fuck you, Dustin!"

"There you go! Incapable of seeing any other viewpoint except your own!"

"You hid this from me for years! How long have you and that old bitch known about Wilson?"

"Don't disrespect my mom!"

"That's right. Noya's so precious. God forbid anyone says anything bad about your *mommy*! You two hid this shit from me for years! You're lucky I don't go to her house and confront her about it."

"Yeah, let your kids see their mom threaten their grandmother. That'll go over real nice."

Wilson opened the car door and slammed it shut. He hated when his parents fought. Michael and Wilson were always getting caught in the middle. He heard the car door open on the other side, and soon Michael was standing beside him.

"This is stupid. Why are mom and dad fighting when they know what's going on?"

Wilson shrugged his shoulders. After looking down the empty dark road for a few minutes, he spoke.

"We have to go back to Grandma Noya's house."

"Dude! Are you serious? That's where the…"

"I know. That's where the entrance to hell is. But that is what the dreams are telling me. It's telling me there's a place for us to hide."

"In Grandma Noya's house?"

"In the house in the forest."

"There? Why?"

"I don't know. There's something about the land that makes it hallowed ground."

Michael twisted his face.

"Hallowed? What does that mean?"

"I think it means blessed."

"Well, whatever it means, you need to tell them so we can go. I don't feel safe here."

Both the boys climbed back in the car. Their parents were still arguing.

"…told you to go off and fuck him!"

"I'm a stranger in my own house!"

"Hey!" yelled Wilson. Both parents turned around to look at him. "Either we get out of here, or something bad is going to happen."

Dustin took a deep breath.

"Where are we going, son?"

"Grandma Noya's. That's what the dream said."

Julia snapped.

"Noya's?! That's the last place I'm going. Fuck that!"

Angrily, she climbed out of the car, slammed the car door, and started walking down the long dark road. Both Wilson and Michael looked at one another in horror.

"Dad! You've got to stop her!" Michael pleaded.

"Get her now!" chimed Wilson.

Dustin angrily kicked open the door and climbed out.

"Julia!" he forcefully whispered. "We need to go! Come on!"

But Dustin couldn't reason with Julia. She angrily walked down the road yelling back at her husband.

"Fuck that! I'm not going to that bitch's house! She's been controlling this family for years! I'll be damned if I go anywhere near her!"

Dustin stopped walking.

"She's dead."

Julia froze in her steps.

"What?"

"She died when all of this weird stuff happened."

"How do you know that?"

"Because she told me it would happen."

"And you believed her? Did you confirm it?"

"No."

"Then how do you know she's dead? She's probably at home drinking tea and laughing at you."

"My mother has been guilty of many things, but she's never been a liar."

Julia started walking back toward her husband.

"Fine! Let's go! I'll bet you any amount of money she's not even dead. It'll be worth it just to show you how much she manipulates you. Let's go!"

Inside the car, Wilson looked at his mother and father's silhouettes, walking back to the car in the darkness.

"Good. Mom and Dad are walking back."

Michael stretched his neck to see his parents.

"It's about time. Why is mom acting all crazy like we did something to her? She's the one that ran off and cheated on Dad."

"She feels guilty, I suppose. It's lonely when you're the only one guilty of crashing the car with everyone inside."

Michael shuddered.

"Dude...you sounded just like Grandma Noya when you said that."

As his parents approached the car, Wilson tapped his eye without realizing it. There was a flash of light, and then he almost screamed. There were thousands and thousands of long-clawed black demonic creatures everywhere. They were all crawling on their bellies towards his parents from both sides of the road. Each monster was hissing and snapping their mouths filled with sharp teeth.

"Holy shit!" yelled Wilson as he opened the car door.

"Mom! Dad! Run!"

Julia was confused and began turning around in all directions. Dustin grabbed Julia by her arm and started running.

"Hurry!" Wilson yelled. "They're right behind you!"

Michael climbed to his knees and looked around.

"What is it? I can't see anything!"

Wilson dove into the front seat and started the car. Just as his parents reached the vehicle, the monsters let out a scream and extended their wings. Thousands of them flew towards the car.

"Dad! We've got to get out of here!"

Dustin peeled out onto the highway, but it was too late. They could hear the thud of thousands of the creatures smashing into the car. Although she couldn't see anything, Julia listened to the monsters' sounds crashing into the car, and she started screaming.

"We're going to die! Oh, my God! We're all going to die!" she yelled hysterically.

"Mom! Shut the fuck up!" yelled Michael. "I've got this!"

Michael turned to his brother.

"Okay, bro. You have to tell me where to shoot."

Wilson shook his head.

"Not on this one, Mike. This time it's all me."

Wilson extended his arms and slammed his hands together. Although he was the only person that could see the demons, everyone in the car saw mounds of black goop splash everywhere. Again, he slammed his hands together, and black liquid covered the windshield.

"I can't see!" yelled Dustin.

"Use the fucking wipers, you idiot!" screamed Julia.

Soon the car accelerated and took off down the road, with Wilson killing the demons on the road behind them.

"Ow! My neck!" screamed Michael. Wilson looked over at his brother and saw three large claw marks on his neck. Suddenly one of the creatures lunged at Wilson, and he ducked. He grabbed the snapping creature by the neck and twisted until the monster's neck broke. Wilson lifted the beast and tossed him out of the hole in the roof of the car.

"Mike! You okay?"

"Yeah. I'll be alright. It's just a scratch."

"My fault. I forgot about the hole in the roof."

Julia had stopped screaming and was staring at Michael's bleeding neck. After looking through the hole in the roof, she gingerly climbed into the backseat and moved between her sons.

"Here, let me take a look at that."

When Julia tilted Michael's neck to look at his wound, she jumped back.

"Ahhhhh!" she screamed. Dustin swerved the car on the road.

"What is it?" he yelled into the back seat. Wilson peered over his mother's shoulder at his little brother's neck. There were hundreds of pulsating bumps covering the area where the monster had scratched him.

"Dustin! We have to get Michael to the hospital!"

"But...I don't know where we are."

"Look! He's going to die if we don't get him to a hospital."

Wilson looked at Michael's face. He was starting to sweat, and his breathing was labored.

"Stop...making such a...fuss. I'm fine."

Dustin slowed the car down and pulled over to the side of the road.

"Wilson. Come with me."

"But Dad! What about those things out there?"

"We have to find some Sage. I know mom taught you about its power, so get out of the car and help me search in the woods."

"But Mom and Mike. They'll be..."

"Get out of the car now, or your brother's going to die!"

Reluctantly, Wilson opened the door and climbed out of the car. Dustin reached into his jeans and pulled out his handgun.

"Here, take this gun. If you hear anything, shoot. You can't see the creatures, but it'll tell us you guys are under attack. We'll rush back to you.

"What?! Are you leaving us here? Are you crazy?"

"I don't have a choice, Julia! Do you want our son to die?"

"No, but I don't want to die either."

Dustin shook his head in disgust.

"We'll be back shortly."

Dustin and Wilson took off into the forest on the side of the road.

"Go ahead and activate the eye," Dustin whispered. Wilson touched his eye and peered into the forest.

"I don't see anything there," Wilson replied. Dustin paused and looked back at the car.

"Look back at the highway and the sky. Do you see anything coming?"

"No. Nothing yet."

"Good. We have three minutes, maybe two. Search over there for the sage. I'll go over to the right."

The two men stepped through the forest, looking at the small bushes and swinging their arms. Wilson was having no luck. All he kept finding was poison ivy. He became nervous that eventually, he would find a snake or a spider.

There was a snap in the woods 30 feet ahead in the darkness, and he paused. Next came another sound of someone stepping on a twig.

"Daaaad," Wilson whispered. "I hear something." Wilson looked in the direction that he had last seen his father.

"Daaad! Come on! Where are you?"

Wilson jumped when he felt a hand on his shoulder.

"I'm here. What is it?" whispered Dustin. Wilson breathed a sigh of relief and pointed into the darkness.

"I heard a noise coming from back there."

"I got the Sage. Let's get back."

Wilson and his father turned and ran back to the car. As soon as Dustin opened the door, Julia fired the handgun into the window. Both Dustin and Wilson ducked as the bullet went flying into the darkness.

"Stop shooting! It's us!" yelled Dustin. Julia angrily tossed the handgun onto the front seat.

"Shit! How the fuck am I supposed to know? Just get us the hell out of here!"

Dustin and Wilson looked at Michael, lying on the backseat. His shirt was wet from sweating, and foam was coming from his mouth. He had large red bumps all over his face. Julia kissed her son and returned to the front seat of the car. Dustin pulled some leaves from the plant and shoved them into his mouth. After chewing them well enough to make them soft, he took the clump of plants from his mouth and shoved them into his son's mouth.

"Can you hear me, son?"

Michael shook his head.

"Chew on this and swallow."

Michael opened his eyes and grimaced.

"Yuck. These plants taste like shit!"

Dustin laughed.

"How would you know? Have you eaten some?"

Michael cracked a smile.

"Such language," complained Julia from the front seat. "When you get better, we're going to need to talk about all the potty mouth. You're too young to be talking like that."

"Mom! I'm sick, and you're talking about curse words?" Michael asked feebly.

"Look, guys, I hate to interrupt you, but we need to go."

Dustin hopped into the front seat and started the car. In a few minutes, they were back on their journey.

29

Changes

"Everyone put on your seatbelts."

The words awakened Wilson and his brother, who was sleeping in the backseat. Their mother, who had also been sleeping, suddenly sat up and pulled at her shoulder harness until it clicked.

"What is it?" asked Michael. Large spotlights were pointing in their direction from the road in front of them.

"It looks like we have some company up ahead. You want to check that out, Wilson?"

Wilson tapped his eyelid and looked ahead.

"I don't see any creatures."

"It must be the military or the police. The cops have blocked the road. Relax. I'll do the talking."

Dustin slowed the vehicle.

"Everybody, stay calm," repeated Dustin.

Wilson could feel his heart thumping through his shirt. There were dozens of men standing in the center of the road wearing hazmat uniforms and helmets like they were taking a trip to the moon. Spools of barbed wire were wrapped around wooden barriers preventing access to the highway. There were dozens of men on both sides of the road with large stationary guns pointed directly at them. Wilson took in small shallow breaths. He had a bad feeling about this.

Dustin pulled up and stopped in front of the closest man to their car. After shining a flashlight into his face, the man motioned for Dustin to roll down his window. He was carrying a laser thermometer with an M-16 slung over his shoulder. Dustin rolled down his window.

"Hello, sir. What's going on?" Dustin nervously asked. The man ignored Dustin and shined a laser thermometer on his forehead. Seconds later, the thermometer beeped.

"May I see some identification, sir?"

"Sure."

Dustin reached into his back pocket and took out his wallet.

"We're just trying to get to my grandmother. She's elderly and…"

Suddenly the officer noticed the hole in the top of the car.

"How did you get that hole in your vehicle?"

"That? I'm not sure how it happened. We were driving along, and we must've hit a…"

"And this sludge covering your car? What is that?"

"As I was saying, we must have run into…"

Suddenly, two other officers approached both sides of the car and shined a light into the backseat. After staring closely at Wilson and Michael, one of the officers pulled out a radio and started talking.

"We have a 10-19 at the 95 South blockade. Send medical personnel."

Dustin was confused.

"Send medical personnel? For what?"

The officer speaking to Dustin took two steps back and raised his weapon.

"Sir! I'm going to ask you to roll up your window. We're going to quarantine you."

"Quarantine? For what?"

"You have approximately five seconds to raise your window, or we will open fire!"

"Okay! Okay!"

Dustin raised the window and moved away from the door. Just as he did, two men moved in with a large machine shaped like a circular microwave.

"What's that?" asked Julia. The man pressed a button, and the machine shot a purple laser into the car.

"I can't see!" yelled Julia.

"Me either!" yelled Michael.

Eventually, the light dimmed, and everyone could see again.

"Oh my God!" exclaimed Dustin. Wilson looked at Michael and jumped away from him. There were thousands of tiny florescent worms moving beneath the skin of Michael's face and neck. Julia turned to look at Michael and vomited into the backseat. Michael glanced from his father's face to his brother's.

"Bro! What is it? What's wrong with me?"

"You're...infected. There are worms everywhere."

Michael started crying and reached out his hand for his mother.

"Mom...please. Help me."

Julia recoiled at the sight of her infected son.

"I'm sorry, Michael. I can't."

Suddenly the car jerked violently. Dustin turned to see a tow truck pulling their vehicle into a clearing on the side of the road.

"What's happening? Where are we going?" asked Wilson. Just as the car descended the small hill on the side of the road, Wilson spotted three men in uniforms standing with flame throwers.

"Dad! They're going to burn us!"

"What?! No! They can't!"

Michael saw the men with flame throwers and fainted. Dustin turned to Wilson.

"Did your grandmother show you all your powers?"

"She told me about some, but there's nothing I can think of that would help us."

Julia was sobbing now.

"It's okay. We'll be okay," Dustin continuously repeated.

Wilson tried to remember everything Grandmother Noya had taught him. He looked at the men standing around their car and tapped his eyelid. The men shot flames of fire at the vehicle.

"NOOOOO!"

There was a burst of blue energy that extended from Wilson's fingers. Suddenly the car was inside a large blue forcefield. The flames from the flamethrowers flew towards the glowing orb. They instantly bent back to the shooters and engulfed all of them in fire. Wilson continued squeezing his eyes closed. Thoughts of flying came into his mind. Slowly, the ball of energy lifted Wilson and his family into the sky. The soldiers on the ground all pointed their weapons at the car and started shooting, but their bullets couldn't penetrate the forcefield. Wilson's power was too great. The ball of energy kept rising until it was towering high in the sky.

"Wilson, are you okay?" whispered Dustin. Wilson's face was pale and sweaty.

"I can't hold on for much longer," he said as both his hands shook.

"Put us down in that field next to the road," instructed Dustin. Wilson opened his eyes and focused on the clearing to the right. He slowly lowered the ball of energy in the clearing and passed out. Just as Wilson did, Dustin started the car and drove onto the road. He knew the police would be coming after them soon and needed to get rid of the vehicle.

30 |

Grand Days

When Wilson regained consciousness, he felt someone pulling him along the grass. He looked up to see his father pulling him by the arm. Wilson looked over and saw Michael lying on a piece of carpet being dragged into the forest by his mother.

"Dad. Let me up," whispered Wilson. His father looked back at him and stopped. Wilson climbed to his feet.

"Mom!" Wilson whispered. "I'll pull Mike."

Julia stopped walking and flopped on the ground.

"Thank God! That boy is freaking heavy!"

The group continued walking until they were half a mile into the forest. Dustin paused briefly and looked back at the road.

"They're not on to us yet. We just need to keep moving."

Wilson looked around, trying to figure out where they were.

"How far are we from Grandma Noya's house?"

"We're not even in Georgia yet. I think we're still in North Carolina. Maybe South Carolina."

Suddenly Julia stopped walking.

"How the hell are we going to get across two states? I'm starving, there are all kinds of weird things trying to kill us, my son is sick, and now the cops are after us."

"I'm hungry too, Dad. Did you bring food from the car?"

"With what's going on with Michael, you sure you want to eat from the car?"

Wilson hadn't checked on Michael's condition since he woke up. He went over to his little brother and leaned over him. Although he was unconscious, the skin on his face shook as the worms moved beneath his skin.

"We've got to get him some help," whispered Wilson. Dustin agreed.

"I know. I just don't know where we can go for something like this."

"AH! What was that?" asked Julia as she pointed into the forest.

"What is it?"

"I saw something moving."

"Everyone be quiet. Don't move."

Dustin stared into the forest.

"I don't see anything. Wilson, what do you see?"

Wilson tapped his eye and looked straight ahead.

"Nothing's there."

"I'm telling you I saw something."

"I don't know…"

Wilson froze.

"I saw something too, Dad. A shadow."

Everyone remained quiet, staring into the darkness.

"Follow me," a voice said from behind them. Julia jumped and fell to the ground.

"Oh, my God! Aaaaah!"

Standing behind Wilson and his family were a large group of children staring with stoic looks on their faces. Some were no more than four years old, and others were teenagers. Most of them held large guns in their hands.

A tall teenager with long blond hair stepped down from his horse and walked over to Wilson.

"Damn. You people are loud."

Dustin walked up to the boy.

"Can you get help for my son?"

The boys walked over to Michael as he lay unconscious on the ground. The boy took one look at him and smiled.

"He got touched by one of the creatures. That's easy to fix."

Dustin's eyes widened.

"Really? How?"

The boy turned and yelled into the group of children.

"Jacob!"

A small brown-haired boy walked up to Michael with a small box. He opened it, took out a fat black leach, and placed it on Michael's cheek. Seconds later, Michael began convulsing, and his body turned black.

"You son of a bitch! What did you do to him?" screamed Julia. Wilson ran to his mother and pulled her away. Wilson and his family stood back and watched as the leech grew before their eyes.

"It's sucking out the infection!" exclaimed Dustin.

Suddenly Michael opened his eyes.

"Grab his hands!" yelled the teenager. Two children ran to Michael and held him down.

"Aaaah! It burns, mom! It burns!"

"Keep him still," yelled the teenager. "If he takes it off, the infection will be permanent."

The leach grew to the size of a baseball as it clung to Michael's face. Finally, after a few seconds, it fell off.

"Grab your son and run! Deep into the forest!"

All the children took off, running into the forest. Dustin grabbed Michael and ran with Wilson and his mother close behind. When the teenager stopped running, everyone fell to the ground.

"Shhh! Nobody says a word! Keep quiet!"

Wilson fell to his stomach and turned around to look in the direction of the leach. What he saw terrified him. Large demonic creatures with red skin began exploding from the dirt in the ground around the leach. They all screamed and fought one another to eat the animal in the center of their circle.

"Oh, my God! What's that?" whispered Julia.

"Demons. They're in the soil. When one of those creatures infects someone, it's like a signal for them to eat."

"Why didn't they get me?"

"The creatures inside your body hadn't hatched yet. They hadn't picked up on your scent."

After a few moments, the creatures seemed to become angry. After growling and biting one another for a few seconds, they dove into the dirt and tunneled underneath the ground.

"Holy shit!" exclaimed Michael. "That was so cool!"

"Michael!" Julia yelled. "That's so cool? You almost died! Stop being an idiot!"

Dustin grabbed Michael's hair.

"You said it burned, but I don't see any marks on your face."

The teenaged boy stood up.

"That's because it didn't hurt him. They make you feel like you're on fire because the creatures are fighting to stay in your body."

The boys turned and walked back to the other children. Dustin chased the boy.

"Hey! We're trying to get to Georgia. Can you help us find a car?"

"Sure. There are a lot of cars. Not much road, though. The military shut that shit down."

"What can we do?"

"Camp out with us until morning. There are some horses on a farm a mile back. You can steal them and cut through the forests."

Julia sucked her teeth.

"Ride a horse until Georgia? Through a forest filled with demonic creatures?"

The boy stopped and turned to Julia.

"Well, you're welcome to get a taxi if you can find one."

The group of children started laughing at Julia. She frowned in protest and turned to look at her sons. They both tried to hide their laughter from her.

As the children continued walking through the forest, Dustin started asking questions.

"Where are your parents? Why are so many of you alone?"

A small child spoke up from behind them.

"I was fishing with my parents when something came out of the water and pulled them in."

Dustin looked at the child in horror. He couldn't have been more than eight years old.

"That's horrible. Did your parents survive?"

"No."

"My brother got eaten by ladybugs," exclaimed a little girl with dreadlocks. "We were out playing in the field when they all rose from the ground and started attacking us. I got away, but the bugs ate the rest of my family."

Another child spoke up.

"I saw a snake eat my grandmother. It grabbed her leg and pulled her down the well. When my granddad tried to pull her up, thousands of ghosts grabbed him and pulled him into the well."

Dustin turned to the teenager.

"So many horror stories. How did you survive?"

"You don't know?"

"Know what?"

"The leader of all of this? It's a little girl."

Hell's Campfire

"Hey man, what happened to your eye?" asked the child with a large bushy afro. Michael jumped in front of Wilson.

"Nothing. What's wrong with your ugly face?"

The child backed away.

"We don't talk to each other like that. Watch your step," said the teenager as he pulled the black child back.

"Settle down, Michael. He was just asking," whispered Dustin. Michael sat down next to Wilson in front of the roaring campfire.

"It's a birth defect that runs in my family."

"Isn't that the truth," Julia grumbled under her breath.

Dustin extended his hand to the teenager.

"How are you doing? My name's Dustin. These are my sons Wilson and Michael. That's my wife, Julia, the polite one."

"My name's Paul, and that's the gang. Say hi, gang."

The kids looked at the family with the same blank looks on their faces.

"You said the leader of all this is a child. How do you know?"

"Little JoJo saw her."

Dustin searched the faces of the children. Finally, his eye fell on the child sitting away from the fire with his gun pointed out into the darkness.

"That's Jojo?"

"Yeah. Jojo doesn't talk much. Ever since he saw the red dogs, he's quiet."

"He saw this child?"

"I did too. JoJo's my kid brother."

"What happened?"

"We were headed to Atlanta to see my cousin. My Dad always liked getting an early start on driving. You know, because of the traffic. Anyway, we're all driving along the road, and it's pretty dark. There was a lot of fog, and my father couldn't see well. Suddenly, we heard this explosion."

"Yeah, we heard it too."

"It was so loud that our windows cracked. Both our ears started bleeding, and everyone in the car started vomiting. The car started swerving, and large pieces of the road just dropped away. Our car fell in. Jojo and I crawled out of the open window to the street. Our parents were unconscious and still in the car. Anyway, we climbed up, and that's when we saw it."

Paul was quiet.

Wilson was impatient.

"What? What did you see?"

"We saw a white wave of smoke approaching us so fast that we didn't have time to react. It knocked us all down. When we stood up, there were spiders all over us. We had them in our hair, clothes, and faces. After clearing away the spiders, I looked up, and there she was. The girl was naked with cockroaches all over her body.

"Shit!"

"That's when the road caved in on our parents and crushed them to death. Meanwhile, the kid just stood there. But she never touched us."

"She didn't?"

"No."

"Why?"

"A couple of cars stopped on the road. People got out and tried to help our parents."

"What did she do?"

"She ran to the first guy and ate the flesh off his face," said Paul.

"My God!" whispered Julia.

"She ripped off the head of the man's wife and started drinking her blood. When the girl finished, there was nothing but a pile of flesh and bones on the ground."

"Holy crap!"

Michael's eyes were sparkling with excitement, and he could hardly contain himself. Dustin patted his son gently on the arm.

"Calm down," he whispered before continuing his questions. "How did you guys manage to escape?"

"The dogs," whispered a tiny voice. The family turned around and looked at the little child sitting away from the group. Paul continued speaking.

"Yeah. The dogs. Hundreds of red dogs came from nowhere. It's like the little girl called them or something. They swarmed around her, but none of them touched her. I tell you, I've never seen dogs so vicious. They were huge with heads the size of truck tires and pitch-black eyes. Before long, another car arrived, and the dogs started smashing their heads against the car. The man and woman locked themselves in the car and refused to come out. That didn't make a difference because those dogs went through the glass to get them. They pulled that couple out and ate them, bones and all. They even ate their clothes. That's when I grabbed JoJo and took off."

"And she let you get away?" asked Michael.

"I wouldn't say she *let* us. More people showed up, and the place turned into a buffet for those things. We just got out of there."

Wilson looked at the boy suspiciously. Something about his story didn't sit well with him. Pieces were missing.

Suddenly, two boys walked up, pulling a medium-sized animal.

"What's that?" asked Michael.

Paul smiled.

"Dinner."

Paul removed a large knife from his hip and sliced it into the creature's flesh. The other children took out knives and started helping in the slaughter. Paul began laughing as Michael and Wilson looked on in disgust.

"Don't worry. We clean and cook the meat."

"Look!" exclaimed a little girl. "I got its heart!"

The little girl held up the animal's heart with blood streaming down her small arms.

"I got its balls!" yelled a boy while holding up the testicles of the animals for all to see. All the children giggled and continued stabbing at the creature.

Wilson became panicked. There was something very wrong with what they were seeing. The brutality at which the children attacked the animal seemed – evil.

"Dad, I have to go to the bathroom."

Dustin looked around and spotted a tree close to the campfire.

"Go behind that tree. I'll be watching you."

"No, Dad. I need all of you to come with me."

Dustin frowned.

"All of us?"

"Yeah. You, mom, and Michael."

"What's going on, son? Is..."

The look on Wilson's face made his father pause. He looked at the group of children attacking the animal and shook his head.

"Okay," said Dustin as he turned to his wife. "Honey, Michael. Come on, guys. We're all going to make a bathroom trip."

"Out here at night? I'm not going out there."

"Come on, Julia. I don't have time for this."

Suddenly all the children stopped hacking at the animal and stared at the family.

"Where are you going?" asked Paul. The boy repulsed Wilson. Blood was all over his face and hands.

"We're going to the bathroom," responded Dustin.

"Bathroom?"

"Yeah. We're all going to pee and then crash around the campfire."

Paul looked around.

"Why don't you just go behind that tree over there?"

Michael interrupted.

"I don't want nobody seeing me pee. Especially a bunch of kids I don't know."

Paul stared at Michael for a few seconds. Finally, he shrugged and stuck his knife in the deer.

"Suit yourself."

Wilson grabbed his mother's hand and pulled her away as Dustin and Michael followed. After they were a few steps from the group, Julia turned to Wilson.

"What is it? What's wrong?"

"It doesn't feel right."

"What do you mean?"

"We've only been seeing these creatures for a few days. Those kids are out here surviving like they were in the forest before this whole thing started."

Julia looked back at the campfire as they walked further away.

"Yeah. Now that you mention it, it was off."

Michael interrupted.

"Yeah, it was weird. A bunch of kids with knives? Where did they get those? They're out here chopping up animals like it's no different than brushing their teeth. I could barely stomach the whole thing. I almost threw up."

Wilson turned to Michael.

"You still have the triangle?"

"In my pocket."

"Good. We might need it. Come on, guys."

Wilson jogged in front of the family as they moved swiftly through the dark forest. Suddenly he stopped. Paul was standing a few feet in front of them.

"Hey. Where are you going? You don't like our hospitality?"

One by one, each of the children stepped from behind the trees to reveal themselves. Dustin nervously spoke up.

"No, it's nothing like that. We just remembered that we need to see about my mother. She's living alone."

This time JoJo stepped from behind a tree and spoke up.

"They're lying. These people don't like us."

Michael moved towards JoJo, but his mother pulled him back.

"Fuck you, runt! Who cares if we don't like kids with knives? If we want to leave, we'll leave."

Paul took a step towards Michael.

"You mean knives like this?"

Paul pulled an enormous knife from the small of his back and held it up. After showing the knife for a few moments, he dropped it on the ground.

"We don't need this."

Paul snapped his fingers, and his whole body ignited in flame. His clothes melted away, revealing reddish skin with tiny reflective bubbles all over it. Suddenly a large horn tore a hole in his face where his nose was, making him gag and laugh at once.

"We don't need silly weapons," he continued in a gargled voice. "We take what we want."

A few of the children screamed and started running away from the group. At that moment, it became apparent to Wilson that some of the children went along with Paul by force.

"There is no escape from hell!" Paul yelled. Suddenly, dozens of demonic birds flew from the trees and attacked the children. Some of the children fought for their lives. They turned and swung at the birds, but there were too many of the creatures. Like a blanket, the birds enveloped the children and feasted on their flesh until their bones were clean.

Jojo changed also. His head began to vibrate wildly back and forth. His neck grew, shooting his head into the trees just above his body. The clothes he wore burned and melted away to reveal rainbow-colored scales all over his torso. Suddenly, there was a loud thud. His head fell to the ground, and his arms and legs fell off his body.

"He's a snake!" yelled Julia. The serpent slithered along the grass and grabbed Wilson by his shoe.

"Hey! Let go of my brother!" yelled Michael. He pulled the triangle from his pocket and aimed it at the center of the snake. A laser shot out of the piece of crystal and split the boy in half.

"Aaaaaah!" the creature screamed as yellow fluid sprayed into the air.

"My brother!" Paul screamed. The demon struggled and removed one of his arms from his body and tossed it at Michael. As soon as the arm touched the ground, it transformed into dozens of large venomous scorpions, all of them running towards Michael. He dove out of the way as several creatures attempted to sting him with their gigantic tails. Wilson saw his opening. He focused on the soil behind Paul just as Grandma Noya taught him. Suddenly two enormous fists made of dirt grabbed Paul and started pulling him into the ground. Paul looked surprised.

"Who are you?"

But Wilson didn't listen. He was too intent on making sure his family could escape. As if he were in quicksand, Paul's body sank into the dirt. As soon as the other monsters saw Wilson's powers, they all sprinted into the forest.

"Now's our chance. Let's get out of here," said Dustin while grabbing his wife's hand. Wilson lifted Michael from the ground, and they all sprinted through the forest.

"You know, I'm still not used to my sons having such power," yelled Julia as they continued to run.

"Me either, but I'm happy they have it," replied Dustin.

As the family got close to the area their car was in, Wilson could see police lights all over the road.

"The cops!" said Dustin. He turned to Wilson. "What now?"

Wilson stopped running and watched as the lights moved back and forth on the road. Finally, an idea struck him.

"Grandma Noya told me I have a power that I haven't tried yet."

"Well? What is it?"

"Teleportation."

Michael looked at his brother.

"You mean like flying hundreds of miles in the blink of an eye? Like the movies?"

"I think so."

Dustin became afraid.

"I don't know about that one, Wilson. What if you make a mistake? One of us could die."

"Then what do you suggest, Dad? The monsters behind us or the cops in front of us?"

Dustin looked at the cops on the road ahead. He couldn't make up his mind.

"I'm with Wilson on this one," whispered Julia. She smiled and pulled her son close. "I just want to get out of this place."

"I'm with you too, bro. Dad, stop being scared. Wilson hasn't failed us yet," whispered Michael.

Wilson tapped his eyelid, held his fingers in place, and closed his eyes. Inside his mind, he visioned standing in the forest behind Grandma Noya's pigpen. Wilson imagined his mother, father, and brother standing in the field by his side. He held his breath and flexed his abdomen while taking all the emotion he felt and pushing it towards his feet.

"Bro! What's happening?" asked Michael. All their bodies began to glow red. Wilson could feel a nauseous feeling in the center of his stomach. He pushed the urge to vomit out of his mind and continued to focus. Dustin wasn't so lucky. Vomit shot from his mouth and sprayed all over the ground. Julia started gagging too.

"I'm going to be sick. Is the onion taste in my mouth a part of it?" Julia asked.

Dustin looked at the police activity on the road.

"Hey!" one of the men yelled. The man removed his machine gun from his shoulder and fired at the family. As the bullets flew by them, Wilson maintained his concentration.

Suddenly a large group of men started sprinting in their direction.

"Wilson, whatever you're going to do, do it now," yelled Dustin.

There was a loud pop and then a crashing sound, like the sound of a firecracker exploding inside a glass jar. A burst of cold wind blew over Wilson's body, and he bit his tongue. After a few moments, everything was quiet. Cautiously, he opened his eyes. He was standing at the edge of the forest behind Grandma Noya's pigpen. He turned to see his family standing beside him.

"Is it over yet?" asked Julia with her eyes squeezed shut. Michael slowly opened his eyes.

"You did it, bro! Holy shit, you can teleport!"

Julia snapped at him.

"Michael! What did I tell you about that cursing? Cut it out. You're too young for that."

The boy ignored his mom and walked to Wilson. Dustin turned to look in the direction of Grandma Noya's house.

"Oh my God," he exclaimed. Everyone turned around to look at Grandma Noya's house – it was gone. In its place was total carnage; a smoldering brick basement, weeds that looked like a giant had smashed them to the ground, and numerous splintered trees scattered around the center of destruction.

Dustin began crying. Julia, remembering the words she said about Grandma Noya, started crying too.

"I didn't know, baby. I'm sorry," she cried.

Dustin exploded.

"What do you mean, you didn't know? I fucking told you!"

As Julia and Dustin fought, Wilson noticed a silvery mist creeping across the ground from where the house was. Michael saw it too and took his triangle from his pocket.

"Mom and Dad, I don't mean to interrupt, but you do realize what's over there, right?"

Dustin saw the mist moving across the ground towards them and wiped the tears from his eyes.

"Okay, let's go."

Wilson and Michael ran into the forest with their parents close behind. Although Michael remembered the fear he'd had of the woods when he and Wilson were there, he buried his fear deep inside and sprinted through the darkness. Wilson tapped his eyelid and looked deep into the forest. There was a glowing light a few hundred feet in front of them.

"Wait!" he whispered to his family. "Hide!"

Julia grabbed Dustin and pulled him behind a tree while Michael and Wilson dove behind a bush. Soon a voice crept out from the darkness.

"How are my grandsons?"

Wilson and Michael frowned at one another.

"Who is that?" Michael asked.

"Did you boys forget about your Grandma Noya?"

"It's my grandma!" Michael whispered to his brother. "But I thought she was dead."

"She is! It's not her," responded Wilson.

"Remember the night we spent in Nana Ama's house? Didn't we have a good time?"

Michael tugged on Wilson's arm.

"Should I shoot her? Just give me the word, big bro."

"No. Don't do it."

Wilson was terrified at what he would feel if he saw his Grandmother. It was a weakness inside himself that he was aware of, and it scared him.

"Julia, is that my son with you?" the creepy voice asked. "Dustin, my son. Come out to see me one last time. Let me feel the heartbeat of my son before I depart this earth."

Wilson looked over at his father. Tears were pouring down his face. Still, he maintained his silence and remained hidden. Michael and Wilson didn't know what to do.

"Why don't you just teleport us out of here? You did it before."

"I don't think I can. I'm exhausted. I don't have the concentration to pull it off."

Soon the white light that was drifting towards streaked across the forest floor and stopped in front of Wilson's hiding place. Michael peeked out from his hiding spot, and a small cry escaped his throat. He started crying and clutching the triangle.

"It's Grandma Noya," he whispered.

"Yes, it's me!" a voice suddenly whispered into Michael's ear. Terrified, Michael screamed out.

"Ahhhh!"

Michael fell on his back and tried to crawl away from the demonic woman. Grandma Noya's eyes were blue flames of fire, and her face had a massive hole in her cheek. Large puss-filled blisters covered her skin, and she smelled of decomposition. Michael gagged and threw up.

Wilson tapped his eye and looked at Grandma Noya. Instead of his grandmother, he saw two beings – the face of an old man and a little girl, sewn together on a woman's body. They were ghosts utilizing Grandma Noya's body to frighten them.

"Come with us! He awaits!" the little girl said.

"He knows of your power. Come with us and help us destroy this world!"

Wilson tried to use his powers to grab the ghosts, but his hand burst into flame. He fell to the ground and threw dirt on it to try to put it out. He quickly tapped his eye and deactivated his powers to see how badly his hand was. It was red and beginning to blister.

"You will come with us! Hell awaits!" cackled Grandma Noya. Dustin ran towards his mother, and she held up one of her arms and tore off her son's right hand. Dustin fell to the ground and began twisting in agony.

"Mom! Why are you doing this?" he yelled. Julia removed her shirt and jumped on her husband. Quickly, she wrapped his wrist in the cloth, took off her belt, and used it as a tourniquet to stop his bleeding. Suddenly, a burst of cold air filled the forest.

"Mike! Get the weapon!" yelled Wilson to his little brother. Michael removed the triangle from his pants and dropped it.

"Fuck!" he yelled as it tried to pick it up again.

"We want to see your soul burn!" a collective group of voices cried out. Wilson watched in horror as the forest filled with hundreds of replicas of his Grandmother, all of them with glowing eyes and pale ghostly skin.

"Wilson! Do something!" yelled Julia. But Wilson was paralyzed. He didn't know what to do if his standard weapons couldn't hurt the ghosts.

"Oh, shit!" yelled Michael as he looked behind them. Dozens of hairless dogs with glowing eyes and snarling teeth were galloping towards their position. Michael aimed the triangle at his grandmother and fired. The woman's body turned gray and fell to the ground with a thud. Two of the ghosts nearest to the two boys screamed and ran to the boys. Michael shot them both, and they fell.

"Come on, Wilson! You've got to help me, man!"

Although the burn on Wilson's hand felt like fire, he raised it. As soon as he aimed it at one of the ghosts, his hand again burst into flame.

"Shit!" he yelled as he threw dirt on it. As soon as the fire was gone, he lifted his hand to look at it. Wilson's hand was blackened and burned. Suddenly, a thought came into his mind. He pushed both hands into the black dirt and focused.

"What are you doing?" asked Michael.

"If I can't touch them, I'll make something else do it."

Suddenly, hundreds of hands burst from the dirt and grabbed the women by their ankles.

"No!" they all screamed in unison. Wilson smiled and focused his energy. One by one, each of the women disappeared underneath the dirt. Michael turned and fired his triangle just as the dogs reached them.

"Bro! Watch out!" he yelled. Wilson ducked, just as a large dog with two heads was about to bite into his back. Wilson activated his powers again and reached out to grab one of the dogs. He was surprised when he caught a three-headed dog and smashed all three heads together, turning the dog into mush. Hundreds of dogs attacked their position, and Wilson began ripping dozens of dogs in half, spraying their blood all over the forest. As he killed dogs by the dozens, he looked back in the direction of Grandma Noya's house. He could see thousands of hellish beasts rushing at them from deep in the forest.

"We've got to get out of here," he yelled. Michael ran to his mother and father and pulled them to their feet.

"Get behind me. Let's go!"

Wilson stood and took off, running behind his family. Dozens of the Grandma Noya replicas attacked them from the treetops. Whenever one flew down to grab Wilson, he dropped to his knees, slammed his hands into the dirt, and pulled the demon underneath the ground. Michael shot dozens of dogs and Grandma replicas as he pushed through the forest.

Finally, the group reached the clearing leading to their Great Grandfather's house.

"There it is!" yelled Michael. "But...what the fuck is that?!"

Wilson looked ahead and saw ghosts standing at the entrance to the property. They were all the ghosts of the slaves he'd seen when he first visited the house. The spirits stared at the approaching family in silence.

"Don't worry about them. The ghosts are part of our family," said Wilson.

"What?"

"Yeah. I saw these guys when we visited with Grandma Noya."

A large dog leaped at Julia. Just as it was about to bite, Julia hit the creature in the mouth with her fist. The dog fell to the ground. Dustin looked at his wife, dumbfounded.

"Where did you learn how to do that?"

"Watching Michael play video games."

Suddenly, Julia saw the ghosts of the slaves waiting for them.

"Dustin! What is that?" yelled Julia when she saw the ghosts.

"Don't worry about them. The ghosts are with us!" yelled Wilson. Dustin grabbed his wife's arm and ran ahead.

"If Wilson says we're okay, we'll be fine."

Suddenly the ground began trembling. Wilson fell to the ground and turned around to look behind them. The remaining dogs howled and scattered in all directions. Wilson could see the shadow of a man with a brimmed hat standing far off in the distance.

"Run!" he yelled. The family sprinted towards their Great Grandfather's house with all their might. Calmly, the shadowy figure strolled behind them. Just as they ran onto the grassy lawn, thousands of the dogs slammed into an invisible wall and disintegrated. The man wearing the hat stopped at the entrance and flashed an evil smile.

Wilson and his family continued running. Michael closed his eyes as his body passed through the hundreds of bodies standing in front of the house. The family made it to the porch and turned around to look at the man watching them.

"Who is that guy?" asked Julia. Wilson knew who he was.

"My guess is that's Mr. Green. He's the man that used to own this place."

Mr. Green extended his hand and pierced the invisible forcefield protecting the land. He smiled as all five of his fingers fell from his hand. His fingers landed on the ground and melted away while the man smiled again, this time holding up his other hand. Suddenly, a red blur of energy appeared beside him.

"What is he doing?" asked Dustin.

Wilson jumped when he saw what appeared beside the man. It was Michael!

Quickly, Wilson looked to his right. Michael was still there. Wilson grabbed his brother and pulled him close.

"Wait! Is that me?" Michael asked. "Fucking cool!"

"Whoa!" yelled Wilson. "Did you see that?"

Both Dustin and Julia moved close to Michael and grabbed him. After they were confident their son was there, Dustin turned his attention back to the man standing on the edge of the forest.

Mr. Green placed his palm over the replica's chest while Michael fell to the ground and screamed, convulsing as blood sprayed from his mouth.

"Michael!" Dustin yelled. "What's wrong, son? What is it?"

Julia yelled at the man standing on the edge of the property.

"Stop, you sick son of a bitch! You're killing him!"

Michael's whole body jerked suddenly.

"Wilson! Kill that fucker!" Michael screamed.

Suddenly blood started soaking through the front of Michael's shirt.

"Where is that blood coming from?" asked Julia as she lifted his shirt.

"Oh, God!" Dustin screamed. Large bubbles began appearing on Michael's chest. As the bubbles grew larger, Wilson could make out shapes in his brother's skin – there were snakes inside of him, trying to get out."

"What...what are those?" screamed Julia.

Wilson began crying in anger as he watched the creatures eat his little brother from the inside. He turned and looked at Mr. Green standing on the edge of the property, holding a replica of his brother with an evil smile on his face.

Wilson felt a wave of anger in him that he'd never felt before. Suddenly both his eyes began glowing red.

"Oh my God, Wilson!" screamed Dustin.

Blood began pouring from Wilson's eyes. A ball of energy formed in his hands, shaking his arms violently. He lifted his arms and pointed them towards Mr. Green. The power exploded from his hand, carving a deep gash in the soil until it reached the man. Mr. Green smiled, and right before the energy hit him, he disappeared.

The Message

Dustin and Wilson lifted Michael and carried him into the old house.

"Michael, can you hear me?" asked Julia. The boy was still conscious but in less pain. The monsters that were in his chest had disappeared when Mr. Green left.

"I'm okay, mom. What happened?"

"That son of a bitch at the forest did something to you."

Wilson moved close to his brother and took his hand.

"You don't remember any of it?"

"I remember looking around at you guys, and then I was dreaming."

"What did you see?"

"Nothing. It was like I was smothering."

"Don't worry about it now, little bro. We're in Great Grandfather Wilson's house. Mr. Green can't come on this land."

"Oh yeah. Grandma Noya said the land is blessed, right?"

"Right. Hey, I'm just going to walk on the porch with Dad to look around. I'll be right back, okay?"

"No problem."

Wilson tapped his Dad on the arm, and they both walked outside on the porch.

"What happened back there with Michael wasn't an accident."

"What do you mean?"

"Remember those kids in the forest that supposedly helped us get rid of those worms inside of Michael?"

"Yeah."

"Whatever they did, they didn't get rid of them. I think the kids activated some process inside of Michael that makes those things grow."

"Are those things trying to eat through his chest?"

"Yeah. It wasn't Mr. Green. The kids did this to him. Mr. Green just called out to those things."

"So, what does this mean?"

"It means we have to find a way to get rid of them, or Michael's going to die."

Dustin looked back at Julia, tending to his son.

"Well, we can't let that happen, can we?"

"No."

"Any thoughts on how we find a way?"

"Yeah, but you won't like it. I have to go after Mr. Green. Alone."

"Alone? Are you crazy? Did you see what he did to your brother?"

"We don't have a choice. Either we go after Mr. Green, or Michael dies here in this old house."

Dustin shook his head in disagreement.

"No. There has to be another way."

"There isn't, and you know it. Don't worry, Dad. Grandma Noya trained me for this."

Suddenly, Michael tried to sit up and winced in pain.

"Lay your little ass back down!" snapped Julia.

"It's okay, mom. I want to sit up for a while."

Suddenly Julia screamed.

"Oh, my God! What is that?"

Wilson and Dustin came running in from outside.

"What is it, Julia?" Dustin asked. His wife could do nothing but point to the chair in the corner of the room.

Sitting in the chair was the ghost of a child, a small Black boy. He dangled his legs on the edge of the chair and chewed on a piece of sugarcane as he stared out past the porch.

"You're going to have a visitor later today. He's coming to help."

Everyone was afraid, except Wilson. He boldly spoke to the child.

"Who is it?"

The little boy smiled.

"You don't need to worry. He's family."

"Family?"

"Yes. He's coming to help you find the buffalo."

"The buffalo? What do you mean?"

The child started laughing.

"You know what I mean. Mr. Green is a bad man. But he is afraid of the buffalo. The visitor will help you find them."

Suddenly the boy hopped down from the chair.

"Yes, ma'am. I'll be right there, ma'am!"

The child took off running and disappeared on the porch.

33

Coming Clean

The sun was rising, and Wilson sat on the porch thinking about what he had to do. He thought about what the child had told him, and he was curious. Who was this visitor? Wilson's family kept so many secrets from him that the possibility of having other family members scattered around didn't seem inconsistent.

Wilson heard footsteps behind him and turned around to see his mother standing in the doorway.

"That floor sure is hard. But we walked to the other room and saw a bed back there. How?"

Wilson smiled.

"Grandma Noya. She put a new bed in here and always traveled here to visit her father."

"Her father? You mean your Great Grandfather?"

"Yeah. Great Grandfather Wilson."

Both Wilson and Julia were quiet as they watched the sunrise.

"You know what's weird? The only time I've ever been awake this early was when I had a briefcase in my hand."

"Yeah, mom. You work a lot."

"Too much sometimes, I think. There are so many things I missed out on by working so much."

"So, why did you?"

"Truthfully? I don't know."

Wilson turned to his mother.

"I know about your abortion."

Julia's eyes widened in surprise. After a few seconds, she dropped her head.

"With everything you and Michael have shown me, I'm not surprised."

"Why did you do it?"

Julia stood up and walked to the edge of the porch.

"Grandma Noya could always see through me. Do you know what she told me the first time she met me?"

"No. What did she say?"

"She told me that I'm carrying a lot of pain with me, and if I don't let it go, I could lose my family."

"Grandma Noya told you that?"

"The first time she met me. Can you believe that? I guess there was something in her that could tell that I was full of shit."

Wilson wiped some dirt off his shoe.

"I guess."

"When I got pregnant, I guess I knew deep down it wasn't your father's. That terrified me, you know? I mean, we already have a family, and I got knocked up by some random fling? There's no way I could make you and your brother go through..."

Wilson interrupted her.

"Michael's not my full blood, is he?"

Julia stared at Wilson for a minute and then sat down beside him.

"Truthfully? I don't know. I mean, I look at Michael, and I look at Dustin. I see father and son. The resemblance is there. And we never had a medical test to confirm it, but I believe Michael is Dustin's son in my heart. And yes, I believe Michael's your full brother. No, I *know* he's your full blood. I don't have any doubt."

Wilson sighed.

"Your guessing doesn't change the fact that you messed up."

"I know. I didn't plan this, you know? Everything just happened so quickly. There's no defending what I did."

"When are you leaving us?"

"Leaving you?"

"That's what your plan was, right? That's why you made Dad beg you to come home."

"Dustin didn't beg me."

"He didn't?"

"No. Your father's a lot closer to Grandma Noya in his behavior. He says things that make you think about your life and the decisions you've made."

"Then why did you come back?"

"Honestly? I love my family."

"So you're not leaving?"

"I never planned to. I did this to get your Dad's attention. He works so much, and he rarely shows what's inside. A lot of what I did was to get his attention."

"Except for the baby."

"Yeah, except for that. That abortion was the biggest mistake of my life. I think about the baby sometimes."

"You do?"

"Yeah. I even named the little girl Dalila. That would've been her name. I've always loved that name."

"You and Mr. McConnell are finished?"

"Do you want me to give you the "nice mommy answer" or the real one?"

"The real one."

"Richard was a pussy. He's not even half the man Dustin is. As I told you, most of what I did was to get your father's attention. But now? Richard doesn't stand a chance."

"Really?"

"Really. Especially after that thing you did with Richard."

"You knew about that?"

"I thought he was losing his fucking mind when he told me how you ripped off his arms and his legs. It turns out the doctors thought he was nuts too. They committed that fool to a mental hospital. I went to Europe alone."

Julia chuckled.

"After all of that crazy stuff at the airport, I knew he was telling the truth."

Suddenly, a flash of light passed in front of them. Wilson watched as the light paused in front of both of them. After a few moments, it moved on and disappeared around the corner of the house. Julia shivered and moved closer to her son.

"I guess I'm not used to seeing all these spirits walking around."

"It doesn't bother me. The spirits are our family."

Julia hugged Wilson.

"Yeah, our family."

34

Shadows of the Night

Dustin came back to the house, carrying two large metal buckets of water. As soon as he placed them on the porch, everyone immediately drank.

"Can you believe mom fortified this place with food? There's even a well out back," exclaimed Dustin.

Wilson's stomach made a loud, growling sound.

"I only wish she had fortified this place with a working bathroom and not an outhouse."

Julia laughed.

"I'm with you on that one, Boy. I can't tell if I'm wiping my butt with paper or poison ivy back there."

Wilson and Julia started laughing.

"Who knew mom was planning for this all along? Can you believe it?"

"I believe it," replied Michael while grabbing a pack of beef jerky. "Grandma Noya always saw more than anyone."

Wilson looked at Michael with suspicion. Although Michael gained most of his strength back, Wilson couldn't help but wonder about the creatures he had in his body.

"How are you feeling, Little Bro?"

"I'm better. Just hungry."

"I'd say. That's your fourth pack of beef jerky."

Dustin felt Michael's head and opened his shirt.

"Well, you don't have a fever, and you don't have any problems with your chest like before. That's a good sign."

Dustin smiled and rubbed Michael's hair.

"The sun's going down now. Maybe we should all try to sleep early. We don't know what tomorrow's going to look like," said Dustin.

Michael yawned and laid down on the floor.

"I'm okay with that. I'm exhausted," Michael said.

"I'll get those blankets from the back," replied Dustin.

As his father walked to the back to retrieve the blankets, Wilson walked out on the front porch. He didn't know why, but something inside of him was restless. Wilson looked out into the dark forest and felt an uneasiness wash over him. He felt nervous, like ants were running up and down his spine. As soon as he sat down on the porch, he understood why.

"You know you're going to have to leave them," a voice said from behind him. Wilson looked and saw the ghost of an old man walk out of the cabin and sit in a rocking chair. Wilson wasn't nervous. He'd seen the spirit before.

"I know."

"Tough decisions always come in the night. They creep in along with the quiet of the morning dew."

"You're my Great Grandfather, aren't you?"

The old man didn't look at Wilson. Instead, he stared out into the forest, ignoring Wilson's direct line of questioning.

"When the Evil One comes for you, accept the invitation. He won't expect it."

"The Evil One? Isn't that Mr. Green?"

"You will need to shed blood to gain the trust of the buffalo."

Suddenly the man stood up and pointed into the forest.

"Look. There! Out past the trees is where they wait."

"Who?"

"Don't be afraid of what he gives you. Focus more on what you can give him. If you do that, you will survive."

"Give him? Like what? A sacrifice?"

The old man finally turned and looked at Wilson.

"Don't worry. Your parents are safe on these grounds. Nothing can penetrate."

The old man walked down off the porch and disappeared. Wilson sat thinking about what he said, not sure of what to make of it. Finally, he stood and went into the house to go to sleep.

35

The Winds Move

Michael woke up in the dark house and looked around.

"Wilson. Do you feel that?" he whispered. No one responded. Michael laid down on the floor and closed his eyes. Suddenly, the whole house shook.

"What's that?" Michael screamed out. He looked around for his family, but he couldn't find them in the darkness. Michael stumbled to the door and looked out into the moonlit yard. Dozens of ghostly spirits were staring at the boy as he tried to gain his balance.

"Help!" Michael cried out to them. "I can't find my family."

The spirits didn't speak. Instead, they all stood motionless, staring at Michael as the house continued to shake. Soon, Michael heard a deep pulsating sound that was like a heartbeat.

"What is that?"

The young boy began to panic. He ran back into the trembling house to search for his family.

"Wilson! Mom! Dad!"

No one answered.

The throbbing sound became louder. The walls of the house began to crack and tilt inward. Michael ran to the porch again.

"What's happening?" he yelled to the spirits. They had all turned their backs to him and stood looking out into the forest.

Suddenly Michael began choking. As he coughed, he could taste a slimy metallic taste in his mouth. He fell down the steps into the yard. The coughing became more intense. Blood oozed from the corners of his mouth as he struggled to catch his breath.

"Wilson, help me," he called out. Suddenly his arm straightened and locked as if he had a metal bar inserted into it. With his free hand, Michael slapped at his wrist, trying to loosen it up. Suddenly, a large worm burst from the palm of his hand. With its long white teeth snapping, the beast twisted its body awkwardly and bit into Michael's chest.

"Ahhhhhh!" Michael screamed. "Mom!"

But no one was around. Michael pulled the worm's mouth from his chest and tossed it into the field. Suddenly, another worm burst from his stomach and twisted itself to bite Michael's chin. Blood sprayed everywhere as Michael fought through the pain and grabbed the animal. He pulled the beast from his face, but not before the animal took a big chunk of his chin with it. Michael fell to the ground and began dragging himself along the weeds towards the forest.

"No. Please stop," Michael begged. The spirits moved out of the way as the child continued crawling towards the forest.

Suddenly, he saw the man standing at the edge of the property. His hand was outstretched as if he were waiting for Michael.

"No!" Michael yelled. He dug his fingernails into the soil and attempted to turn around to go back to the house. But he couldn't move. It felt like something was pulling his body along the ground against his will. Suddenly Michael stood up. He tore off his shirt and screamed. The mouths of hundreds of worms pressed against the inside of his chest and back. All of the creatures were trying to eat their way out of his body. Two long worms burst from his chest and burrowed into the dirt. Michael fell, and the serpents pulled him along the soil towards the forest. Unable to resist anymore, the child blacked out.

36

Michael

"Waaaake up!"

Wilson sat up immediately and looked at the front door. The spirit of the little Cherokee girl he'd seen when he first came to visit his Great Grandfather was standing in the doorway screaming at him.

"Heee leaves! Gooooo!"

Wilson looked around the room and saw his mother and father sleeping in the corner.

"Where's Michael?" he whispered.

The spirit became louder and more vocal.

"Gooooo!" the little girl screamed.

Michael took off, running out the front door. Just as he ran down the stairs, he saw his brother at the edge of the yard.

"Michael!" he yelled. "Stop!"

His brother stopped walking and turned around to look back at the house. That's when Wilson saw him: Mr. Green. The man's eyes glowed red, and his arm extended in the direction of Michael. Blood was pouring from Michael's eyes, and two large serpents hung from his chest into the soil.

"Let go of him!" yelled Wilson, his mother and father running behind him. There was a flash of light, and both Mr. Green and Michael were gone.

37

Going After Michael

"No! You can't go!" yelled Julia as she pushed Wilson away from the door.

"I don't have a choice!" Wilson screamed. "That's my brother out there, and I'm the only person that can bring him back!"

Wilson grabbed a few packs of beef jerky and shoved them into his pockets. Julia turned to Dustin.

"Dustin, do something! You just can't let him go out there. You saw what happened to Michael."

"I agree with Wilson. He's the only person that can get him back."

"Am I the only person that saw what that man did to our son? When are the two of you going to get it through your heads that this is a fight Wilson can't win?"

Wilson paused.

"Gee, thanks for the vote of confidence, Mom. It's good to know I have your support."

"Don't do that, damn it! Don't turn this into some show of whether I support you. I just saw our son getting eaten alive by snakes, serpents, or whatever those damned things were. And nobody could do a damn thing about it."

Wilson walked close to his mom.

"Why don't you say what you're thinking?"

"What do you mean?"

"Go ahead, say it."

Julia remained silent.

"Fine. If you don't say it, I will. You think that it's better to lose one son than to lose them both. That's what you're thinking, aren't you, Mom?"

Everyone was silent.

"Yeah. I thought so."

Wilson walked out of the house and into the yard. As he started to walk to the forest, his father yelled to him.

"Wilson! Wait!"

Wilson turned and waited for his father to arrive.

"I understand the reason you have to leave. I do."

"Why can't Mom? She acts like there are other options."

"I think she understands the reason you have to go, but you need to understand her position as well."

"What do you mean?"

"She's a mom that just had her child taken away from her in the worst way imaginable. Try being sympathetic to that. It's not easy being a parent."

"And it's not easy being a son."

"Nobody is saying it is. But you need to be respectful of a mother's love for her child. You don't have a right to tell her how she should love her children."

Wilson thought for a moment. Maybe he was wrong for the way he spoke to his mother.

"Look. Go out there and bring your brother back. And protect yourself also. We don't want our family any more stressed than it already is."

Wilson hugged his Dad.

"Remember. As long as you and mom are on this land, you're safe. Grandma Noya made sure she had enough supplies to last for a while. I shouldn't be too long. You and mom can use this alone time to try to fix a few things between you."

"That's going to be hard when our children are missing, and the spirits of the dead surround us."

"You'll find a way."

Dustin smiled.

"Sure, we will, Son. Sure, we will."

38

The Warriors

As Wilson walked to the edge of the forest, he paused. He saw what looked like several spirits standing there waiting for him. There were a young African American boy and two Native American boys. But these spirits seemed different because they didn't have the same mystical glow as the others. These spirits seemed – real.

As Wilson walked closer, he heard the boys speaking to one another.

"Is it him?"

"Yeah. That's Wilson."

"I thought he was going to be bigger. He doesn't look like much."

Finally, Wilson stopped just in front of the spot where he'd last seen his brother.

"Who are you? What do you want?" Wilson asked as he stared at the boys suspiciously. The black kid spoke up first.

"I'm Tariq. I think you're my cousin."

"Cousin?"

"At least that's what my mom told me."

The two other boys spoke up.

"I'm Takatoka, and this is Calian. We're your cousins too."

"So, I'm just supposed to accept three strange kids that show up claiming to be related to me as my family?"

Tariq spoke up.

"You can accept what you want. But we live in the world just like you do. And if we don't find a way to deal with what's happening, we're all dead."

"How did you find me?"

"The same way you knew we would come. The spirits told us."

Wilson walked past the boys into the forest.

"Thanks, but I don't think I need your help. You'll slow me down."

Calian started laughing.

"What's so funny?"

"You. You're acting like a real dummy now. Didn't you lose your brother to that evil man? And you don't need our help? Who are you fooling?"

"Well...I don't need your help. I can protect myself."

This time Takatoka spoke.

"We know about your powers, but do you know about ours?"

Wilson was surprised. He hadn't considered that the boys had something worthwhile to contribute.

"What can you do?" asked Wilson.

"I have the power to disappear," replied Takatoka. "I can also make animals do what I want."

Wilson turned to Tariq.

"And you? What can you do?"

"I can speak to the spirits."

Wilson turned to Calian.

"What can you do?"

"I ain't telling you shit."

"What?"

"This ain't no fucking job interview. I can take care of myself. That's all you need to know."

Wilson smiled. Calian's sharp tongue reminded him of his brother Michael.

"Fine. But I'm not babysitting any kids. If you can't protect yourself, you get left behind."

Wilson started walking through the forest.

"You know, you don't have to act like an arrogant prick about this. We are your family, you know," said Takatoka as they walked behind Wilson.

"We need to work together, guys. Like it or not, we all live in this world. And if we don't stop this demon from taking over, we're all dead."

As the group of boys disappeared into the forest, the spirit of the old man stood watching them until they were gone.

"That's a strong group of hunters. Too bad one of them will die before the second sunset. If only they knew what the Evil One had in store for them."

www.ingramcontent.com/pod-product-compliance
Lightning Source LLC
Chambersburg PA
CBHW060414310726
48976CB00003B/1050